# ROMANCING THE OMEGA

## HOBSON HILLS OMEGAS: BOOK THREE

### C.W. GRAY

# ROMANCING THE OMEGA

Hobson Hills Omegas: Book Three
By C.W. Gray

❃ Created with Vellum

Caden stared around the crowded bookstore. It was larger than it looked from outside. Two large bay windows overlooked the cold, wintery streets of Hobson Hills. Inside, cozy reading nooks contrasted with the iced-over glass panes. There were several other seating areas throughout the open space, but Caden was drawn to the two next to the windows.

The store was organized chaos with books, comics, and interesting odds and ends. The owner had created a children's section with books, toys, and kid-sized seating. It was separated from the rest of the store by a short white picket fence. He even spied a closed-in play area for toddlers. He imagined busy parents would love to put their kids down in a safe place, then peruse the store on their own.

Today was the opening day for The Book Worm, and it looked like most of the town was there to get a look. Zoe Wilson had convinced the new owner to go in with her to make a wide archway in the wall it shared with her bakery, Honey Buns. Now, on a cold spring day, a person could grab a coffee and Danish, then go buy a book.

If they felt like visiting with friends, they could grab a table in the bakery. If they wanted more privacy, they had their choice of several comfortable chairs and couches spread throughout the bookstore. If he wanted to get out of the house and work on his next novel, this would be the place, surrounded by books and the smell of coffee and baked goods.

"Caden, move your ass," Grey said, pulling his arm. "I want to sign up for the book club before it fills up."

"Surely there won't be that many people interested in a book club in rural Maine," he said, tempted to roll his eyes.

Someone bumped into him. The woman's apology froze on her lips once she spotted the rabbit strapped to his chest like a baby. She blinked a few times then abruptly turned and walked away. Huckleberry had convinced Caden to take him this morning. Sassy had wanted to sleep, and his Huck was lonely. The Book Worm was pet friendly, so he didn't understand why people kept staring at him. Grey carried his son, Rue, in a baby sling too. People were strange.

Grey grabbed the sign-up sheet and held it up beside his smug face. "There's twenty people already, Caden, so I'm signing us both up. They'll probably let you bring Huckleberry too. I can't believe you bring him everywhere." He shook his head. "That is one spoiled bunny."

"Sassy sleeps a lot, and Huck is a people rabbit. He

needs to be with his person," Caden said, turning to scan the crowds.

Grey replied back, but Caden didn't hear him. He didn't hear anyone. He didn't see the crowd full of Wilsons, Bensons, and more. All he saw was the angel at the register, patiently talking to a customer. He was simply breathtaking. The omega looked Korean-American, and his black hair was fine and shiny, falling loosely around his face. His black eyes danced with humor as he spoke, waving his hands. His face had a pointy little elf-like chin, adding to the air of mischief that surrounded him.

The man's eyes found his, and they seemed to stare into his soul. Caden panicked. He ducked behind the nearest bookshelf, breathing heavily. Huck wiggled his nose and watched him as Grey followed behind, frowning.

"What the hell are you doing?"

Caden ignored him, peeking around the shelf. The omega looked straight at him, brow raised. Caden ducked behind the shelf again. Oh fuck. What was wrong with him? This wasn't like him at all. He was stoic, well-mannered, blah, blah, blah. He wasn't some teenager, hand pressed against his beating heart, trembling from seeing his first crush. Fuck. He removed his hand from his chest and ignored the pounding of his heart.

"Caden, who are you hiding from?" Grey looked around the shelf. "Why is the owner smirking our way?" He ducked back beside Caden and stared at him. "Caden, do you *like* him?"

Caden turned around, leaving Grey, and started walking down the aisle. If he ignored the situation, it would go away. That always seemed to never, ever work. Fuck.

A small figure popped up right in front of him, startling him. A little boy, maybe two years old, stood staring at him. He had to be related to the angel. He had the man's eyes and his little pointed chin. He sucked on his thumb, eyes glued to Huckleberry.

He held his arms up to Caden, eyes beseeching. "Up," he said. "Bun bun."

"Linc, what are you doing?" A young girl scooped the boy up.

The toddler ignored her and reached out, placing his little hands around Huckleberry's ears. His giggle was infectious.

"Sorry about him," she said, laughing. "I'm watching him, but he moves so fast."

Grey smiled. "Hi, Summer."

"Hey, Grey," she said, trying to contain the wiggling boy.

"Hannah was just telling me about your ice-skating trip."

"It was really fun," she said, blushing at the mention of Hannah. "I only fell three times, but Hannah says I fall with grace."

Grey laughed. "This is my best friend, Caden, and I guess this little guy is Linc? Hannah mentioned him."

"Yeah. He's my nephew," she said.

"Is your brother the guy at the register? I haven't met him yet," Grey said.

Caden hid his surprise. Summer didn't look anything like Linc or Caden's angel. Grey slid him a look, and Caden knew he was in luck. Grey could do the whole chitchat thing, so he could get what Caden needed. He knew there was a reason he loved the guy.

Summer nodded. "We just moved here from Tennessee, so we haven't met a lot of people yet. Linc, what is wrong with you?"

Linc decided he wanted Caden, and he wanted him right then. He leaned out of Summer's arms and grabbed Caden's shirt. The toddler kicked back with his legs, and Caden caught him up in his arms to keep the boy from falling.

"Tennessee? Wow. That's awesome," Grey said, trying to keep Summer talking. Linc wasn't helping the cause.

"I'm so sorry about him," she said, trying to pry the boy away. Linc held onto Caden's shoulder and Huck's sling with an iron grip.

"He's okay," Caden said. "He likes Huckleberry."

"Where's this little guy's other parent? I'm trying to put together a daddy's club," Grey said.

Summer smiled gratefully at Caden, then looked back at Grey. "My brother is divorced. He's an omega, but he married a woman. Now he's a single parent. I know he'd love to have support from other dads."

Grey looked straight at him. "Aww, a single dad. Single."

Caden swallowed hard. Single. Oh god, the angel was single. This was it. Wait, he was also previously married to a woman. Hmm.

"I know Yeo plans on having a daily children's story time. I think he'll meet a lot of other parents there too," Summer said. "You should bring your son. He's tiny, but it couldn't hurt, right?"

"Now there's an idea," Grey said, stroking Rue's head. "You could spend some time with your unofficial nephew. What do you say, Uncle Caden?"

"I could make the time," Caden said casually. His heart sped up at the thought of being close to Yeo. His name was Yeo. He sighed, and Grey snorted. Summer watched him curiously.

"Bun bun," Linc said, petting Huckleberry.

He laid his head on Caden's shoulder, and Caden's fast-beating heart melted. The kid was so damn cute.

"Bun bun," the little boy repeated with awe.

"Linc," Summer said, holding her arms out. "Come on."

The boy ignored her.

"We can watch him," Grey said. "We were just going to walk around the store."

"Are you sure you wouldn't mind? Yeo could probably use some help at the front," Summer said. "We haven't had time to find an official sitter. You're one of the few people I know here, and Yeo is an extreme homebody, so he knows even fewer people than I do. You wouldn't think it to see him at work, but once he's done for the day, he doesn't leave the apartment."

"We won't mind a bit," Grey said. "Come on, Caden. Let's go look at the comic books."

They threaded through the crowds. Summer ran to the front, and Grey smirked at him as he thumbed through the comics. "I knew he was divorced, you know. I was just asking for you."

"How did you know?"

"Hannah and Summer are good friends, and Summer confided in her. I'm not one to spread gossip, so I didn't say anything to anyone." Grey looked around. "There are a lot of alphas here today. I wonder if they're checking out the new omega."

Caden panicked, spinning around in circles and counting the alphas.

Linc giggled. "Whee."

"Oh my god, you have it bad." Grey started laughing and didn't seem inclined to stop.

"What's so funny?" Caden's brother-in-law, Elijah, asked as he reached them. His daughter, Olive, ran around the store, admiring everything. The girl loved reading, and Caden knew he'd be buying his niece some books today. He might even buy one of those Harry Potter wands she was currently staring at. He had to keep an edge to stay the favorite uncle.

"Caden is in looove," Grey said, drawing the word out. "He has the hots for Summer's brother."

Elijah looked at him, eyes wide and glistening. His smile was luminous. "Really?"

*Pregnant men are ridiculous,* Caden thought. He watched the hearts fill Elijah's eyes and sighed. God help him.

"Caden, dear." His mother, Susan Benson swept in, kissing his cheek. "Who is this darling little boy?"

"This is Linc," he said gruffly. "He belongs to the bookstore owner."

"Love bun bun and Cay Cay," Linc said, smiling at Caden's mom.

Grey and Elijah leaned on each other.

"Aww," they said in unison.

"Did you hear that?" Grey patted his eyes with his sleeve.

"He said he loved Caden," Elijah said, lip trembling again.

"No, he didn't," Caden said, trying not to roll his eyes like a heathen. He spent way too much time with Grey, Justin, and Abel. "He's a baby. Don't put words in his mouth." He turned back to his mom, the sanest of the three people in front of him. "How do you like the bookstore?"

"It's charming," she said. "I can see your father and me spending a lot of time here when we're in town." She smiled wickedly. "Your father is taking the opportunity to buy all your books while we're here. We have a set of them back home, but he wants a set for the vacation house too."

"I think he's why my book sales have rocketed," Caden said wryly. "Does he know that he doesn't have to buy books he probably won't read, just because they're mine?"

"Not at all," Susan said. "Besides, I love Roxanne Baxter, so they *will* be read."

"The better question is: does he know he doesn't have to buy them eight hundred times," Elijah said, laughing. He pointed at the front of the store. Caden's dad had several copies of each of his books.

"He likes to give them as gifts," Susan said, giving a delicate shrug.

"Yes! Look, Caden. I found a set of Starfire comics," Grey said. He bounced in place as he stacked up eight comic books. "It's the whole set, and I've been looking for them forever."

"Starfire? Pink hair? Teenager?" Elijah looked confused. "You like her comics?"

"Not that Starfire," Grey said. "This one is a badass from the seventies. I wanted to get a set of them for Olive. Starfire will be a good role model."

"The cover has a woman pointing a sword at a man's throat, saying *'you dare ask for mercy,'*" Caden said. He thought for a moment. "I agree. Olive needs those."

He snuggled Linc closer and flipped through a different box of comics while Grey and Elijah argued. He picked up some Spider-Woman and Captain Marvel comics too. He grabbed the pile in front of Grey and added the Starfire comics to his own selection.

"Come on, buddy," he said to Linc. "Let's go look at the kid's books. I bet we can find some fun stuff to read."

He left his arguing friends and pushed through the crowd to the kid's corner. Olive already sat in a comfy, kid-sized chair, book in her lap. Several other kids ran around the area or sat and played with the toys.

"Uncle Caden," she said, jumping up. "What are you looking for? I can help."

"Linc and I want to read a book. What would you

recommend?" He set the boy on the ground. Linc promptly grabbed his leg, refusing to let go. Caden laughed as he unstrapped Huckleberry.

"*The Cow Said Neigh* is a good one," she said. She pulled it off the shelf and handed it to him. "Can I read with you?"

"Of course. You make the sounds. Okay?" He kissed the top of her head, and they settled into a corner filled with large pillows. Linc and Huckleberry cuddled in his lap, and Olive leaned into his side. Several of the kids turned their attention to him and crept forward so they could hear the story too. A little red-headed girl around Linc's age plopped into his lap, squishing Huckleberry between her and Linc.

*This is a perfect moment,* he thought. Just a few months ago, he had been so unhappy that he had wanted to just disappear from the world. Now, he was settling into a damn good life. Hopefully, it was a life an angel would be interested in. He needed to think carefully about his courtship, so he would get it right. He was a romance author. How hard could it be?

"There once was a cow in a barn," Caden started reading. "Who could see a horse in a field."

# CHAPTER 2

*Y*eo watched the beautiful, blond woman kiss the handsome alpha's cheek. Linc smiled at the woman, then snuggled against the alpha's chest. Yeo's shoulders slumped even as he carried on his conversation with his customer. Of course an alpha that handsome and that sweet would be married. It wouldn't matter even if he was single, Yeo reminded himself. He pinched his leg behind the counter and told himself not to be an idiot. A handsome face meant nothing.

"There's already thirty people on the book club list. Do you think I should sign up with that many?" The woman in front of him looked disappointed.

"Of course you should," Yeo said. "After we have a final number of participants, I'll split them into smaller groups. The best book clubs are the cozy ones."

The woman smiled. "Perfect. I'll go sign up now."

She finished paying and grabbed her bag, running back to the sign-up sheet.

"I'm surprised a book club is that popular here," a man said. He was older, but very attractive. In fact, he looked a lot like Mr. Handsome. The man stacked several copies of each of Roxanne Baxter's novels on the counter. Yeo blinked at the stacks, then shook his head. If he had steady customers like this, The Book Worm would turn a hefty profit for sure.

"I think it's more the socializing part of it," Yeo said. "We'll talk about a book, yes, but we'll also have snacks, drinks, and good company. Are you interested?"

He rang up the books, eyes widening at the total. The man just handed over his card, completely unconcerned about the bill.

"My wife and I are only in the area about once a month, so she was hesitant to sign up," the man said. He pointed at the beautiful blond. "She loves reading, though, so if you don't mind a few absences from her, I'll tell her to go ahead."

"She's your wife?" Yeo frowned. Why was she kissing Yeo's alpha if she was already married? Fuck. Not. My. Alpha. It was just the baby fever talking, and maybe the way Mr. Handsome held Linc in his arms. Steady and safe.

"Yes," the man said. "My name is John and she's Susan. Our son, Caden, is around here somewhere."

"Son?" That would explain it. Good. Yeo wouldn't have to break the man's heart by telling him his wife was a hussy.

"Caden is a good man," John said, patting his bags of books, his eyes full of pride. Damn. It must be nice to have a dad like him.

"I think he's the one watching my son for me. Hmm, now that I say that aloud, I think I should probably go find the little imp," Yeo said. The line had shortened just a bit, so Summer should be okay on her own for a few minutes.

Summer snorted. "If he's a friend of Grey, then he's good. Trust me."

John laughed. "I think Caden headed to the kid's corner. I'll walk with you."

Yeo followed the man, and they had to push through the crowds. If he were alone, he'd do a little happy dance right now. He hadn't expected such a good crowd, even on opening day. The kid's corner was full of toddlers and younger kids. Parents stood around, talking to one another and keeping an eye on their children. Yeo's son was currently sleeping on Caden's chest with a little red-haired girl. They hugged a very hairy rabbit between them. Caden's deep voice flowed over the children gathered around him to listen to the story he read.

Yeo held in his sigh of pleasure. While this was just about the most adorable thing he'd ever seen an alpha do, Mr. Handsome couldn't be perfect. If he'd learned anything from his family, it was that alphas couldn't be trusted, even if this one looked absolutely perfect holding his son. He would make a wonderful dad. Yeo pinched his leg again. Damn baby fever!

Caden finished the story, and the kids surrounding him slowly moved away. The older girl curled into his side grabbed his book and added it to a small pile next to him. "We need this one too, Uncle Caden. You never know when you'll need a book to read to a baby."

"Olive, darling, you have your Uncle Caden wrapped around your little finger," John said. Caden looked up, his brown eyes widening when he saw Yeo. John held his bags and smiled down at his son. "You look comfortable there. Thinking about giving me more grandchildren? You're already thirty-four, and you're not getting any younger. When is the last time you went on a date?"

"Father," Caden said, voice scandalized. Yeo couldn't stop his smile.

"Uncle Caden, do you have to poop? You look like you have to poop," Olive said. She put her head on her uncle's shoulder and scrutinized his face.

"Hi," Yeo said, stifling his laughter. "I'm Yeo Cook. That's my son you have there. I'm sorry you got stuck with him."

"He's fine," Caden said, blushing. He looked down at Linc. "I like him." He looked at the little red-haired girl. "I have no idea who this is though."

Yeo smiled. "I'll take Linc and put him in his nap roll behind the register."

He leaned down and picked his son up.

"Bun bun," Linc said sleepily. He fell back asleep as soon as his head hit Yeo's shoulder.

"I think he loves my rabbit," Caden said, blush deepening. He tried to get up, but the other toddler was still sleeping, and Olive still lay against him.

"He can't possibly love that thing more than you," John said. "I can't believe you carry it around in a baby sling, son. You are far too attached to that rabbit. You really need to date more before you become the weird man with fifty rabbits."

"Father," Caden said again, a slight whine in his voice.

Yeo hid his smile against Linc's soft hair. "I'll just put Linc down. Thanks, Caden."

He made himself walk away. Caden looked like he wanted to follow, but he was trapped. His eyes followed Yeo all the way to the front of the store, and a shiver ran up Yeo's back. He laid Linc in his nap roll. It was light purple and covered in rabbits. Linc did love his bunnies. He latched the baby gate, closing in the register area.

Summer smiled and said goodbye to her customer, then turned to Yeo. "He was nice, right?"

"He was," Yeo said. He was fucking perfect. He smiled at the next customer and began ringing up her books. The line had grown while he was gone. It was going to be a wonderful, busy day. Maybe he had done the right thing in moving to a tiny town in Maine. He just had to keep away from Mr. Handsome before he did something stupid.

"I can't believe so many people came," Summer said. She moaned as she took off her shoes at the door to their apartment. They lived in the spacious apartment above the bookstore, making the walk home blessedly short. "You did good, Yeo."

"I did well, sweetie," he corrected absently. "Not good."

He set Linc down and watched his boy toddle across the hardwood floor. The boy went straight to his toy kitchen and started banging the plastic pans around.

"I have to admit that this town surprised me. We'll have to split the book club into four groups."

"You'll still have story time every day too. We're going to be busy," Summer said. She didn't sound displeased. The couch pulled her in when she plopped down. "Oh my god, it feels so good to sit."

"Thank you for your help, sweetie. You know I don't expect you to slave away in the bookstore every day. You have a life to live."

The teenager rolled her eyes. "Don't be stupid and say no to free labor."

"Hmm, you make a good point," he said, throwing a pillow at her. The apartment was good sized. He had bought the store and living space and had completely remodeled the apartment and bookstore both. It may have taken months, but their home looked good.

The apartment had a master bedroom and bath, along with three smaller bedrooms and two more bathrooms. The walls were brick and covered in colorful paintings. The living room and kitchen were completely open, letting Linc get everywhere he wanted, good or bad. Their furniture was durable, comfortable, and brightly colored. Large bay windows overlooked the street and a fireplace warmed everything. Photos lined the mantle, and he'd hung strings of colored glass from the ceiling. The light made the room a million shades of color. It was the perfect home for his little family. He thought of the gated community he'd left in Tennessee. He didn't miss it a bit.

Yeo's phone rang. He looked at the number and sighed. "Hey, Fawn."

He pretended not to hear the growl from the couch.

"How is she doing? Did her first week of classes go alright?"

"She's doing fine. She's made some friends, and the town isn't too bigoted for a queer thirteen-year-old," Yeo said. He smiled at Summer's laugh.

"Yeo," his stepmom said, exasperated. Yeo found it hard to hate her. She had taken him in and raised him as her own, even though he was physical proof of her husband's infidelity. Granted, her way of raising kids tended to be very hands off. Nannies were the norm in the Cook household.

"Do you want to talk to your daughter?"

"I had best not," Fawn said worriedly. "You know how Michael is."

"I do," Yeo said. His dad was garbage, pure and simple.

"I'm sending some more money orders," she said. "How's your new place?"

"We like it," he said. He still needed to put the money orders from last week into Summer's college fund. "Today was opening day for The Book Worm, and we did really well. It was a promising start."

"If anyone would know how to run a business, it's

you," Fawn said, pride in her voice. "Your father isn't happy with the man he hired to replace you."

"Is that glee in your voice, Fawn?" Yeo laughed and sat on the couch beside Summer.

"Serves him right," she said. "You were running the company just fine, and he had to go and ruin it."

"I'm surprised Derek didn't step in."

"I love my son, but he just doesn't have a head for business. Of course, you can't tell him that," Fawn said. "Well, your father *did* tell him that, but he thinks Michael just hates him." She gasped. "Oh, I meant to tell you. I didn't want you hearing it from somewhere else. Derek is dating Tracy."

Yeo winced. "Why would she do that to herself? Wait, why would he do that to himself?"

"That ex-wife of yours is all about image, and right now, the eldest grandson of Richard Cook gives her quite the boost in society."

"Yeah. That sounds like her," Yeo said. He looked at his son playing at his toy kitchen. Tracy hadn't wanted to ruin her figure having a baby. He sure as shit hadn't minded getting pregnant himself, even if she had insisted he hide it from everyone. "Has Papa called? My birthday was two weeks ago, and he always calls on my birthday."

"No, darling. I haven't heard from him. I have your new number to give him when he does call. You know he will. Oh dear, I need to go," Fawn said quietly. "He just got home." She was silent for a minute. "Tell her I love her."

"I'll tell her, but it would mean more coming from

you." She hung up without replying, and Yeo sighed. Complicated woman. Summer was curled into a ball, earbuds in her ears, music blasting. He went to the kitchen and started dinner. "You okay with chicken stir-fry?"

"Yeah," Summer said. Her head peaked over the couch, earbuds gone. "I noticed you were acting kind of weird about Caden. Do you not like him? I thought he was nice."

"He seems nice," Yeo said, wincing.

"Somehow, I'm not reassured," Summer said drily.

"He's an alpha," Yeo said.

"Not all alphas are like Dad, Derek, and Grandpa. Hannah's alpha dad and her oldest brother are super nice. Their omegas seem really happy," she said.

"I get it," he said, sighing. He stirred the vegetables in the pan. "It's just hard to trust people. I was never encouraged to talk to other omegas to hear it from them, so it's hard to picture alphas being nice." He looked at her. Her light brown hair and hazel eyes were all he could see over the couch. "That's why I'm so proud of you, Summer. You look for the best in everyone, no matter what. You're so brave."

"Brave got me kicked out," she said. She lifted up and crossed her arms on the back of the couch. "It also got you divorced and disowned."

"Your bravery is the best thing that ever happened to me," he said, giving her a pointed look. "I wish it were easier for you, but our life here is already ten times better than my life with Tracy."

She gave him a small smile. "It's better here for me

too. I don't have to avoid Dad and Derek or go to any of Mom's stupid parties with boys she *approves* of. I do miss Lowell."

"Me too." Yeo's youngest brother was so sweet. For now, at least. Give it a few years, and their dad would ruin Lowell too. "I miss Fawn too. She loves you."

"She didn't stop him from kicking me out. They signed me over to you, Yeo," she said. "I love you so much, but they just signed me over like I was a plot of land."

"She should have stood up for you, but that's not her way, sweetie."

"I know," Summer said. "She's the Queen of Passive Aggressiveness." She looked at him, watching him as he cooked. "Promise me something, Yeo."

"Anything, sweetie."

"Promise me that if you come across an alpha that you like, you'll give him a chance."

"That's a hard thing to ask, Summer."

"I know it is," she said softly. "Promise me anyway."

Yeo thought of big, brown eyes and a sweet blush. "Okay. I promise."

# CHAPTER 3

Caden walked around Farm Fresh. Huckleberry was riding in his baby sling, and Sassy walked beside him on her leash. The three searched the store, looking for the perfect gift for Yeo.

"Caden?"

Elijah's aunt came to stand beside him as he eyed a bunch of Ernie's scarves. It almost physically hurt to consider buying the man's homemade, knitted scarves. He was one of Carter's best friends, and Caden was irrationally jealous of the omega. Caden and Carter were brothers, so they should have been best friends. They had never been close as kids, though, and that distance followed them into adulthood. *Carter sure found it easy to make friends wherever he goes,* Caden thought sourly. Fucker.

"Anna," Caden said, nodding. "I'm looking for a gift."

She put a hand on her hip and eyed him. "A gift? Would it be for a certain bookstore owner?"

"Who told?"

"My Eli-baby tells me everything," she said, smirking. "He also told me your idiot father completely embarrassed you in front of Yeo."

"He did," Caden said, eyes narrowing. He would have his revenge.

"Well, how about a pretty scarf to start? What about this bright red one or maybe this dark teal one?"

"The teal one is pretty," he said reluctantly. It really was nice, damn it. "What about something of Harper's?"

Caden *liked* Harper. He was Grey's alpha.

"I know! I know," she said. "What about a set of Harper's bowls? They're hand-carved maple."

"I like that idea," he said. "They're beautiful too."

Harper always tried to make his crafts special in some way. The set of bowls had flowers carved onto the sides of them.

"I'll bag them up for you. Wait. I better wrap them. Men never seem to take that last step." Anna took her time wrapping the bowls in tissue paper and taping them. She did the same with the scarf, then set them all inside a large, plain brown paper bag, adding some more tissue paper to the bag. "There we go. It's basic, but better than just handing them over."

"Thanks, Anna. How much do I owe you?"

"Seriously?" She looked at him as if he were crazy. "You're family, Caden. You don't pay in money. You pay in labor. Spring is coming. Be ready."

"Why do I feel like I'd rather pay with money?" The Wilson family ran a large farm, and every last one of them worked their asses off. Hard manual labor wasn't Caden's thing.

Anna smiled sweetly and patted his cheek. "Don't you worry, baby doll. We'll go easy on you this first time."

Caden left the store and drove to town. There was still a bit of a crowd at The Book Worm. It had been open for a few days now, but the town was small and it was winter. A group of older women and omegas sat in chairs towards the back. It looked like the first weekly book club meeting. The book for this month was a light read – a romance about an omega and an alpha by Roxanne Baxter. Caden strongly felt Grey and Elijah had something to do with that.

The line died down, and Caden took a deep breath and stood in front of his angel.

"Yeo," he said, then stared blankly at the gorgeous omega. He blinked. Yeo blinked. They stared for a few minutes. "I got you a gift."

Caden pushed the bag toward Yeo. The omega stumbled back a bit, startled.

"Thank you, Caden. You didn't have to do that," Yeo said with a hesitant smile.

"It's no big deal," he mumbled.

"Cay Cay?" Linc poked his head over the baby gate that closed in the back area of the register. "Bun bun?"

"Hey buddy," Caden said. He looked to Yeo. "Can I put Sassy and Huckleberry back there, so Linc can play with them? They're both really good with kids."

Yeo smiled wide, black eyes sparkling. "That would be great. Linc loves animals, especially rabbits."

Caden froze, unable to move. Yeo's smile was so damn sweet.

"Caden? Back at the bookstore again?" His dad came to stand by him, and Caden almost winced. "Don't you work, son? I know reading is important for your job, but you don't need to get lazy. Routines are important."

Great. Now it sounded like he just lazed about all day.

"I see you brought the rabbit again. Son, you're never going to meet an omega if you're carrying a rabbit around like a baby. They'll think you're weird."

A giggle escaped Yeo, and his wide eyes met Caden's. He gave in and rolled his eyes, pleased to hear another giggle. He picked up Sassy and put her in with Linc, then unstrapped Huck and set him down.

"Bun bun," Linc said and plopped down on his butt to play with the rabbit. Sassy licked his face, and the little boy laughed, hugging her around her neck.

Caden turned and walked toward the door to Honey Buns. "Come on, Dad. I'll buy you a coffee."

He loved his dad. He really did.

"That's wonderful. We don't talk enough since you moved," John said, following him into the restaurant to wait in line. "That new man Cain hired is doing great. Plus, Smithson stepped right into your cases, and everything has gone smoothly so far."

"I'm glad," Caden said. "I felt so guilty for leaving, but I just couldn't do it anymore. I didn't want the quality of my work to start deteriorating."

"Don't worry about it," John said. "You're happy and relaxed now. You're still quiet, but it's a peaceful quiet."

"I love writing," Caden said.

He ordered a mocha, and his dad ordered a plain, black coffee. They sat at a table near the bookstore entrance. Caden could just see Linc through the gate. Yeo was rifling through his bag of gifts.

"How is Grey's case going?"

"It's just a few days away, but they're well prepared. The man will pay," Caden said. Grey's former supervisor had tried to kill him multiple times. He had blamed Grey for getting fired.

"Good," John said. "The case against the institute in Nevada is also progressing well. Noah isn't the only one who wasn't there voluntarily."

Caden started to nod, then stilled. He grinned. Yeo had wrapped the scarf around his neck and pulled it up to cover the bottom of his face. His eyes were fixed on Caden and were filled with joy as he danced in place. He must like the scarf.

"There is something I've been meaning to tell you," John said. Caden turned his attention back to his father. "Your mother and I are thinking of moving here permanently. Cain is happy as a clam in Georgia, but he's not ready to settle down yet. Olive and the twins are here. Well, the twins will be here in the summer."

"You would actually retire?" Caden was shocked. His father loved the firm.

"Yes," John said. "I would still go to Georgia once a month to touch base with Cain and our clients, but I would be officially retired."

"I never thought I'd see the day," Caden said. "Are you sure it's what you want?"

"I am," John said, voice full of certainty. "It's time to focus on your mother and the grandchildren. It doesn't hurt that you're here too." John leaned forward. "I should warn you, son. Your mother has decided you need an omega."

Yeo caught his attention again. He held one of the bowls up. He looked at Caden, then pointed to his chest and mouthed *mine?* Caden nodded, and the omega started dancing again.

"Hmm, maybe your mother won't have to worry about finding you an omega," John said, amused. He looked between Caden and Yeo, and Caden couldn't stop his blush.

Caden tried to give his father a stern look. "I won't stand a chance with him if you keep embarrassing me in front of him."

"Embarrassing you? How have I embarrassed you?" John asked.

Caden stared him down.

"I can tell you how you embarrassed him," Zoe Wilson said, plopping down into Caden's lap. "You were a typical dad. I swear, parents are oblivious, aren't they? God, my feet hurt. Why did I open a damn bakery again?"

"Because you love it," Caden said. He'd grown used to Zoe and her ways. It reminded him why he had never wanted a sister. "Father is worse than a typical dad. He says all the wrong things."

"I don't know what you mean," John said. "I'm perfectly eloquent."

Caden yawned. "You're fine, Dad, just try not to mention my lack of dating and general laziness in front of Yeo, alright? That should do it."

John winced. "I don't think he's too worried about what I've said now."

Caden looked at Yeo. The man was glaring at him. He took off his scarf and stuffed it in the bag. Scowling at Caden, he tossed the bag into the garbage can next to the register. Caden rubbed his chest, hurt. What had he done wrong?

"Son, don't look so heartbroken," John said. "You can certainly fix this. Just push Zoe off your lap and explain to your omega that she's basically your little sister."

"Oh god," he said, pushing Zoe off him. She landed on her feet, but just barely. "I didn't even realize what it looked like."

"Oh man," she said. "I'm sorry, Caden. I'll go fix him his favorite drink and get him a muffin. Go apologize. Now!"

Caden rushed to the register and had to wait while Yeo rang four different customers up, his expression frosty. He didn't even look at Caden.

"Cay Cay," Link said, smiling up at him. The little boy leaned back against Sassy and waved at him. His dog was napping. Again. He held Huckleberry in his lap.

"May I help you?" Yeo's voice was as cold as his

expression. The other customers were gone, each giving him sympathetic looks as they left.

"Zoe is disgusting," he said quickly.

Yeo gasped, going from frosty to pissed off.

"Really, Caden? Really?" Zoe stood behind him, holding a latte and a banana muffin. She handed it to Yeo. "I swear, for a suave lawyer, he sure puts his foot in his mouth around you, Yeo. What this idiot is trying to say is that we aren't romantically involved. He's like a brother to me. I'm used to sitting on him all the time."

Yeo's anger faded, and he turned red. "Oh."

"This is my apology," she said, motioning to the coffee and muffin. "You two had better talk."

She turned and strode back to her bakery.

Yeo looked at Caden, tears in his eyes. He wiped his hands across his cheeks angrily. "You shouldn't be all perfect and make me like you if you're already dating someone."

His lip trembled, and Caden's heart about broke.

"I'm sorry, Yeo. I really didn't think about how it looked." He thought for a minute. "Wait. I'm not dating Zoe. You heard her, right?"

"We saw Zoe in your lap, and Mrs. Haverty told me you were seeing three different omegas. She said you even go out with all three sometimes." A tear fell down his cheek. "You shouldn't have been nice to me, Caden. It's not right." He growled. "Damn baby fever. That's what this is. I don't like you."

"Baby fever? You want babies?" He was a little embarrassed at how eager he sounded. "Wait, three omegas? What in the hell is she talking about?" He thought for a minute, and his eyes widened as he realized what it was. "Oh. She must mean Grey, Abel, and Justin."

"You forgot you had three omegas?" Yeo stared at him in hurt disbelief. "Is this some kind of sister wives thing?"

"They aren't my omegas," Caden said, laughing. "I can't wait to tell them about this." He made sure Yeo's wet eyes were watching him. "Grey is married to Harper. Justin is dating a cop, and Abel is like Zoe. He's basically my little brother. They all are. They're my best friends, so we go places together all the time."

"You're friends with omegas?" Yeo watched him curiously. "You're not like any alpha I've ever met."

"Hobson Hills has a lot of good alphas," he said, then realized what he said. "None are as good as me though. I'm the best and the most handsome, so don't go looking at them." He pressed his face into his hands. "I can't believe I just said that."

He couldn't bear to look at Yeo's face, so he ran out the door, forgetting about Sassy and Huckleberry.

For two hours, Caden walked up and down the cold streets of Hobson Hills. He couldn't bring himself to go back inside the bookstore to get his pets. Yeo had to think he was either an idiot or a pompous jerk.

"Caden? What are you doing pacing the streets?" Gramps Wilson was a tall man with white hair and kind eyes. "What's wrong, son?"

"I'm an idiot," Caden said. "I don't know why I like Yeo so much, but being around him turns me into a complete nincompoop."

"Yeo, huh? Elijah told me you fancied an omega here in town." He watched him with amusement. "The romance novelist can't figure out how to romance his omega?"

"Don't laugh," Caden said. "Writing about love is much easier than feeling it."

"Don't I know it," Gramps said. He wrapped an arm around Caden's shoulders. "Listen. No one and nothing is perfect. You're going to say stupid things. He'll say stupid things. There will be miscommunications and misunderstandings all around. The important thing is that you don't run from him. You don't give up on him. Well, unless he tells you too. Don't be a stalker, son."

Caden's lips twitched. "We haven't even really talked yet. I can't even get to that point."

"When I met Laurel for the first time, her and her friends were swimming in the lake. I thought I'd impress her, so I jumped in, off a cliff. I lost my shorts," Gramps said. "I've never been so embarrassed in all my life. That water was cold, son."

Caden laughed. "Really? That happened?"

"Yes," Gramps said. "I didn't give up though." He eyed Caden. "You haven't lost your pants yet, so you shouldn't be so worried."

"Alright," he said. "I need to go get Huck and Sassy anyway. I left them in there."

Gramps chuckled and gave him a little push. "Get moving."

Caden walked back into The Book Worm and stood awkwardly at the register. Yeo eyed him as he worked with a customer. Caden noticed the bag of gifts wasn't in the garbage can anymore, and the scarf was once again wrapped around Yeo's neck. Linc was napping in his nap roll. Huckleberry and Sassy's heads both poked up out of the roll too, right next to his.

"Forget something?"

He turned to Yeo, blushing. "A few things, really. I'm glad Linc likes animals. Does he have a pet? He's so gentle with Sassy and Huckleberry."

"We don't," Yeo said. "My parents never let me have any pets and my ex-wife hated animals. I've always wanted a pet, and I know Linc would love one too." He shot his son a fond look. "One day."

"I'm sorry I'm an idiot around you," Caden said.

"Well, I'm an idiot around you too," Yeo said, softly. "Did you forget I actually cried when I thought you were dating someone else? We're even on the embarrassment level."

"Where does this leave us then?"

"You know where I work, right?" Yeo smiled shyly.

Caden grinned. "Yes," he said. "I do."

"We'll start there."

# CHAPTER 4

A few days later, Yeo chatted with a customer and kept an eye on the man settling into the chair in front of the window. He was too pale.

"Do you think there's any room for me in one of the book clubs?" The middle aged woman nibbled her lip. She held the Roxanne Baxter novel clutched to her chest. "I know they've started already, but I can catch up."

She looked emotionally beat down, as if a giant stood atop her every second of every day.

"Of course, there's room for you," Yeo said, smiling. He thought he knew the best group for her too. "Can you do Wednesday evenings, around five?"

Laurel Wilson and Ines Torres would take this woman under their wings. If there was a way to help her feel better, they would find it.

"Wednesdays would be fine. Can I bring anything? I heard there were food and drinks."

"Anything you want," he said.

"My son always says I make really good peanut butter cookies," she said, eyes wide with excitement.

"That sounds delicious," he said.

"I'll do it," she said, voice firm. "Thank you."

She took her bag and walked from the store with a bounce in her step.

Yeo looked around, happy for a minute of peace. Linc was napping, so he could take a look at the shelves. The whimper to his right froze him in his tracks.

"Oh god, not now," the man by the window said.

He jumped up and ran toward the bathroom. Yeo followed, worried about the man. He heard retching through the door. Oh, dear.

He ran and grabbed a bottle of water, checking the front for customers. By the time the man came back out, Yeo had served two more customers and made a small plate of crackers.

"Sir, are you alright?" Yeo walked around the register and handed him the water and crackers.

"I'm so embarrassed," the man said. He took the water and plate and sat in his seat. "Thank you so much."

"How far along are you?"

"You can tell I'm pregnant?" The man looked shocked. "Only a few of my family members know. The others haven't noticed a thing."

"Did you want them to notice? It's pretty easy to hide as long as you're not puking," Yeo said with a smile. He had gone for almost five months without anyone noticing when he was pregnant with Linc.

"I don't know," the man said, wrinkling his nose. "I know what they'll say. I'm in my forties and have three kids. Why did I want more?"

"Why wouldn't you?" Yeo sighed, dropping into the chair across from him. If he could, he'd have a million kids.

"That's what I'm saying," the man said, voice rising. "I love kids. I'm a stay-at-home dad, and I miss having babies around. I don't want to have more *me* time. Harper is grown and married, with a baby of his own. Shawn is about to move out and start his own life. I have Hannah, but she's thirteen."

"Those names sound familiar," Yeo said, musing.

"Oh, I'm so sorry. My name is Bennett Wilson. Summer is friends with my daughter, Hannah."

"Ah, that's it," Yeo said. "Well, if you want a baby, it shouldn't matter to anyone else. It's not their business."

"Oh, I know. I just love our extended family so much. I hate to disappoint them," Bennett said.

"Would they really care that much that you're having another baby?" Yeo's experiences with the Wilsons had been great so far.

"Probably not," Bennett said, sighing. "When I talked about wanting to, Anna, my sister-in-law, said I should think about it more. Barry, my brother-in-law, said I was crazy, but that's just Barry."

"How did your alpha feel about it?" Summer had said that Bennett's alpha was a good man.

Bennett grinned. "Marco is my cowboy. He will give me anything I want as long as it makes me happy. He doesn't get why I'm keeping it secret."

"Well, there you go. That's all you need." Yeo sat back. "Your family is pretty amazing, you know? Summer absolutely adores you all."

"She is a good girl," Bennett said, munching on a cracker. "Can I ask you about her parents? She hasn't said anything, and I didn't want to press her. I imagine she talks to Hannah a lot, but Hannah doesn't share secrets."

"My dad and stepmom found out that she likes girls, not guys. They didn't handle it well," Yeo said. "The Cooks of middle Tennessee are conservative and traditional. Women marry men, omegas don't exist, and the wife stays out of the husband's business. My dad wanted Summer gone. My stepmom wanted her somewhere safe, so she talked my dad into signing over custody to me. Of course, I was happy to have her. I love my sister."

"That poor girl," Bennett said. "I can't imagine not accepting any of my children."

"You're okay with Hannah then? Summer seemed to think she was worried about it."

"Okay? With what?" Bennett looked puzzled. Oh fuck a duck.

"Nothing," Yeo said quickly. "Nothing at all."

Bennett's eyes narrowed. "What do you know?"

"It's not my secret to share. It's nothing bad. I promise," Yeo said.

"Hmph," Bennett said. "It's not dangerous?"

"Not at all. She'll tell you when she's ready."

"Okay. I *can* respect my daughter's privacy. I can." He shook himself, then turned his attention to Yeo.

"So… Caden?"

"How do you know about him?" Yeo tried not to blush. He wore his new scarf again. It made him happy to look at it. So what?

"He's an honorary Wilson. Plus, it's not like he's been subtle in his awkward courtship."

"His courtship is just fine," Yeo said happily. "I've never been courted before, and I like that he's honest in his reactions. He is definitely not smooth and practiced." He sighed. "I really like him, Bennett. I haven't had good experiences with alphas though."

"He is a good man," Bennett said. "He might seem standoffish at first, but I've seen him with his niece, Olive. He has a good heart."

Yeo shouldn't care what Bennett thought, but he was relieved to hear another omega's thoughts on the alpha he was so interested in. "He's really good with Linc too." Yeo nibbled his lip. "I heard his dad say something about him being a lawyer?"

"He was a lawyer for a long time, but he made a career change. He still helps the family out when we need it, but he doesn't actively practice anymore." Bennett smiled at him. "Don't you think you should talk to Caden about Caden?"

"He's not here, is he?" Yeo pouted, then shrugged. "Tell me more about this baby you're having?"

Between serving customers and taking care of Linc, the two men talked for a few hours. Yeo had never had a friend before. He checked the clock. "I can't believe it's already three in the afternoon. Summer will be in soon."

Bennett held Linc on his lap. He had just finished reading him a Dr. Seuss book. "Good lord. I've had way too much fun with you."

He set Linc down behind the register and returned the book to Linc's book box.

"See you tomorrow?" Yeo held his breath. He really liked Bennett. His father had chosen the people he could call *friends,* and, needless to say, they weren't really friends. He wanted Bennett to like him, almost as badly as he wanted Caden to fall in love with him.

"Of course," Bennett said. "I'm working a few hours at Farm Fresh in the morning, and I'll want a cozy place to rest my feet. If I can have a cute, little Linc in my lap, all the better."

Yeo waited until Bennett left to do his happy dance. He had a friend. God, he was such a dork.

A few customers later, Summer came through the door. She peeked in at Linc and gave Yeo a kiss on the cheek.

"Did you eat lunch today?" She eyed Yeo as his stomach growled.

"I forgot," he said. "I really need to hire another person."

"I've got the perfect person in mind," Summer said, smiling excitedly. "Hannah's cousin, Olive, is best friends with a little girl named Shelly. Her mom does seasonal work for the Wilsons, but she's been trying to find a full-time job. There aren't a lot of opportunities in Hobson Hills. A lot of the people here work in different towns."

"Get her number and I'll call her," he said.

"I'll text Hannah now, but you need to take a break and eat." She pointed to Zoe's bakery. "Go."

Yeo sniffed. "Bossy." He picked up Linc and tickled his son's belly. "You got your lunch, didn't you? Bennett took good care of you while papa was too busy."

Yeo really needed to hire someone. His son needed more of his attention, especially if he ever hoped to finish potty-training him.

He ordered a latte and a sandwich, then sat in Bennett's chair by the window. Linc walked around unsteadily, giving every item in his path his undivided attention. Summer darted over and put a few toys on the floor.

"Stay here and relax a bit," she ordered him.

Yeo stuck his tongue out at her but did as he was told. He watched the people bustling back and forth in the cold and smiled when he saw Caden. Mr. Handsome carried a plant in a deep teal pot. The plant was covered in wrapping to protect it from the cold, so Yeo couldn't tell what it was. In his other arm, he had a basket filled with something. It was covered with another scarf, red this time.

Yeo finished his sandwich and went to open the door for him.

"I was hoping you would come by today," he said, smiling at the alpha.

Caden blushed. Damn, Yeo liked his blushes. They looked so out of place on his strong face.

"I brought you some things." He held the basket and plant out to him.

"Come sit with me."

He pulled Caden to the cozy little reading nook Yeo had spent so much time in that day.

"You don't have to bring me presents every time you come by, Caden." Yeo took the basket and plant. "Not that I mind. Is that another scarf? I thought it looked like one."

He set them both on the small table between the three chairs. Linc plopped down on the floor and played with the stuffed, velveteen rabbit in front of him.

"You smile when I give you gifts," Caden said and sat. "I really like your smile."

Yeo couldn't stop his grin. "Bennett told me you were a lawyer for a while. Why did you change careers? That's a lot of time spent in school to choose a different path."

Caden looked thoughtful. "I didn't mind it at first. Law isn't something I'm passionate about, but you don't have to be passionate about your job, right? It made my father so happy."

"I guess if your career is just a job, that works," Yeo said. "Lots of people work to make money to survive."

"Yeah," Caden said. "With the firm, though, I worked sixty to eighty hours a week. It came to be that was *all* my life was. Then, I found something I really liked. Something that I love with every fiber of my being."

"What is it? Bennett wouldn't say."

Caden blushed red. "I'll tell you another time. Okay? It's kind of embarrassing."

"You don't have to tell me a thing, Caden. Whenever

you're ready, I'm right here." Yeo couldn't help but wonder what kind of career would be embarrassing. He didn't want to push. There was plenty he didn't tell people.

"I will," Caden said. "Soon. Anyway, when I found my real calling, working at the firm made me feel like I was being pushed into a tiny room that I couldn't leave. It was suffocating."

"I know what you mean," Yeo said, sighing. "I'm glad you quit. How did your family handle it?"

"That's why it took so long to leave. I thought my father and brother would hate me. I feel like such an idiot now. My whole family fully supports me in every way. I was just too caught up in my self-doubt to see it," Caden said. "My father may have a habit of embarrassing me in front of you, but my mother and him love me."

"I could tell he does," Yeo said. "It's obvious in how he looks at you. That is one proud papa."

"When I made the announcement, it seemed natural to move here from Georgia. Carter, one of my brothers, lives here with his omega and daughter."

"Are you two close?"

"Not really," Caden said. He shook his head. "I thought the move would change something between us, but so far it hasn't."

"Hmm. Maybe you two need to spend more time together, get to know each other," Yeo said.

"Maybe. What about you? What made you want to open a bookstore in rural Maine?" Caden's eyes were warm, and Yeo wished he was sitting on his lap like Zoe had.

"I was the CEO of Cook Enterprises. They're a big deal in the south," Yeo said.

"I've heard of them," Caden said. "That's a big change. Really big."

"I hated it," Yeo said. "Every second of every day was a performance. Someone was always watching, so I had to act a certain way all the time. I could never be me. Hell, sometimes I don't even think I know who *Yeo* is."

"Why did you do it?" Caden moved to sit on the coffee table. He took Yeo's hand in his.

"You wanted to please your family, right? For the longest time, that's all I wanted. I wanted my grandpa and dad to be proud of me, to not regret me. If it took pretending like I wasn't an omega, marrying a woman I hated, and working at a company I abhorred, that wasn't important," Yeo said.

"What changed? With me, it took being at my lowest and having the support of some good friends," Caden said.

"Summer happened," Yeo said. He watched his sister talk to a costumer at the register. "My parents couldn't accept who she is. They signed custody of her over to me, but my dad couldn't take it. The way it looked to other people. He fired and disowned me, my wife divorced me, and I finally, *finally*, got to be free. Lord, those were the best things to ever happen to me. I wish I had been strong enough to leave earlier."

"Your father is an idiot. I heard a lot of things about that company, and they were all good."

Yeo grinned. "They are having some problems adjusting. I don't regret leaving though. I got a top notch severance package and this place. You have no idea how much I love this place."

Caden smile was lopsided. "I can guess."

"You're already here," Grey said, running through the door. "It's book club time." The omega waved a worn copy of the Roxanne Baxter novel. He stopped moving and stared wide-eyed at Caden's face. "Holy shit! You're smiling."

"Uh oh," another omega said, following Grey over to their corner. This one was blond and very pretty. Yeo fought his urge to growl at the man when he put his hand on Caden's shoulder. "Were we supposed to bring gifts for the host? I didn't bring anything."

A third omega pushed the blond away from Caden. "Seriously, Abel? That's Caden's omega."

"Oh," Abel said, sending Yeo a devious look. "I see how it is."

"I seriously doubt you do," the third omega said. He rolled his eyes and waved. "Hi. I'm Justin. This idiot is Abel, and you've met Grey. We're Caden's harem apparently."

"Sister wives forever!" Abel threw a fist in the air. "Oh, hey there, cutie."

Linc looked at the three omegas, then turned to Caden. "Cay Cay, up!"

"Aww," the three omegas said together.

Caden ignored them and picked Linc up.

"You all can sit wherever you'd like in that back corner," Yeo said, pulling himself together and standing. "You have about fifteen minutes before the discussion starts."

He looked at the covered tray in Grey's hands. "I see you brought some snacks. Feel free to put them on the coffee table in the center."

"Are you going to join us?" Caden asked hopefully.

Yeo nudged him with his shoulder, smiling sweetly. "I wish I could, but until I hire another person, I have to watch the register all the time. I'll be watching, though, so you better behave."

The three omegas pulled Caden to their corner, and Yeo reluctantly made his way back to the register with his gifts. "Damn it. I forgot Linc again."

Summer laughed and handed a customer her change. "He looks perfectly content where he is." Caden watched him from his seat. He hugged Linc to him and mouthed, *mine*. "See?"

"You may be right," Yeo said. "Caden didn't bring Sassy or Huckleberry. He probably needs something to hug."

"Sassy and Huckleberry would be less stinky," Summer said. She started poking the basket. "What you got there?"

Yeo finished unwrapping the beautiful fern. He set it on the corner of the register and admired it. "That's so pretty."

"Yeo," Summer said. "What's in the basket? I need to know."

"You are so impatient," he said and gently removed

the beautiful scarf from the top, setting it aside. He would be wearing it tomorrow. Nestled within the basket were two glass bottles of milk, a large hunk of butter, a small loaf of honey oat bread, and a dozen blue eggs. Yeo smiled at his alpha's choice of courting gifts.

"Bread, eggs, milk, and butter? Does he want you to make him breakfast?" Summer looked confused. "That's not exactly a romantic gift."

"No. It's not romantic. It's Caden. He's my thoughtful alpha," Yeo said, watching Caden as the book club officially started. He shook his head and smiled. "I don't want normal, Summer. I want Caden Benson."

# CHAPTER 5

"**Y**ou gave him eggs and milk? Are you crazy?" Abel looked at him in disbelief. "Do you want him to make you a cake? Think romantic, Caden. Romantic!"

"He really liked it," Caden said sullenly.

"Do you want him to be your friend or your omega?" Justin asked. "Roses, chocolates, or lacy underwear are the way to go, big guy."

Caden blanched. What would Yeo think of him if he gave him lacy underwear? Hmm, Yeo in lacy underwear.

"No," Grey said. "Gifts need to come from the heart. You know what Harper got me? Tiny, Opal, and Butterball." He stopped at his car and unlocked the door. He looked back at Caden. "Do what your heart tells you, Caden."

What the hell kind of advice was that? His heart was telling him to follow Yeo around all day, every day, learning everything he could about the beautiful man. Caden didn't want to go to jail.

"Sure," he said when Grey kept staring at him, waiting for an answer.

"I mean it." Grey stomped his foot. "Don't worry about what anyone but Yeo thinks. If you want to give him cakes and brownies and Amish cheese, then that's what you give him."

Caden raised a brow. It sounded like Grey was hungry.

"Don't show off your brow. That's not nice."

Caden barely resisted the urge to roll his eyes. "Goodnight, Grey."

He waited until he got into his car and started it, then walked Justin to his.

"Roses, chocolates, and lacy underwear," the man said. "That's romance."

He unlocked his Jeep and got in. One more omega to go.

Abel watched him as they walked to his car. "You really like this guy, don't you?"

"I've never felt this way," Caden admitted. "As soon as I saw him, I knew he was someone special."

"Everyone is someone special," Abel said. "Yeo's kind of special just meshes well with yours."

"Huh?"

Abel rolled his eyes and ignored Caden's eloquence. "He reminds me of you. Yes, he smiles and laughs and dances, but there's something about him that reminds me of you." Abel leaned back against his car, thinking.

"It's like he's a kid seeing his first rainbow. There's awe and appreciation for every detail."

Caden stared at him, surprised at his insight.

"He's just now free to be himself," Caden said. "His life has been a lot like mine only he didn't have good parents."

"That makes sense," Abel said. "You remember how I made you go to the movies every day for two weeks last month?"

"How can I forget? It was a zombie marathon. I filled a room at the cabin with canned goods and tooth paste. Thank you for my new paranoia."

Abel giggled. "You're welcome. Anyway, the reason I did that is because of the look on your face. It's like you had never taken the time to do something so silly."

"I hadn't," Caden said. "It was fun."

"Maybe, think about some things that Yeo hasn't been able to do and help him do it."

"That's a really good idea," Caden said. "Thank you, Abel."

Abel unlocked his door. He patted Caden's cheek. "You'll do good, big guy. Good luck."

He started his car, and Caden watched him drive away.

"What is something Yeo wants, but hasn't gotten yet?" Caden grinned. He knew exactly what to do.

"ARE you sure you want this one?" Dr. Grover asked.

"He needs a good home, and he *is* a big sweetheart, but he's huge."

"He's perfect. Grey says Maine Coons are gentle and lazy cats," Caden said. Huckleberry watched the large Maine Coon cat from his sling on Caden's chest. Sassy sniffed at the cat. The big feline sniffed back, somehow managing not to move. There was no doubt that the cat was big. He was easily twice as big as Grey's Maine Coon, Tiny. He had long, grey and white hair with solid black stripes. His chest and his front right paw were pure white. He really was perfect.

"An animal shelter a few towns over was on the verge of putting him down, since he had been there so long. I had the room, so I took him. I had planned on conning your brother into taking another pet, but I'll save him for another time," Dr. Grover said.

Caden couldn't stop his grin. His brother really was a big softy. "What should I buy at the pet store?"

"Litter, food, dishes, a bed, and toys." The veterinarian pulled a ragged stuffed squirrel out from under the beast. "He loves this thing, so you'll be taking it with you." Dr. Grover gave him a stern look. "If your omega decides he doesn't want this big fella, what are you going to do?"

"He'll want him," Caden said with certainty. "However, if he completely surprises me and doesn't want him, I'll take him. He'll have a home, doctor. I promise."

"Good man." The doctor smiled and petted Huckleberry. "I think you're as big a softy as your brother. Now, what's this I hear about you having a harem of omegas? Are you adding poor Yeo to your harem?"

"Really, doctor? Really?" Caden sniffed. "You should know better than to listen to gossip."

"This gossip is so funny though." Dr. Grover chuckled as he loaded the big cat into a cat carrier. "In all seriousness, good luck with your courtship, son."

Caden left the veterinarian and his laughter behind and made a quick trip to the pet store. He looked in the back seat. "I don't want to leave you in the car and take the others. That doesn't seem fair."

The cat's grey eyes met his through the bars of his carrier.

"I can't do it." He dug around in his glove compartment and found one of Sassy's extra leashes. "Let's see if this will work." He opened the carrier and fastened the leash on the collar. The cat just stared at him. He strapped Huck into his sling and grabbed Sassy's and the cat's leashes, letting them hop out of the car. Sassy followed right behind him, but the cat just sat on the cold cement. "Come on, buddy."

"Caden? Are you trying to walk a cat?"

Caden grimaced at the voice. He really didn't want to talk to Juan. The man was another one of Carter's best friends. Juan, Ray, and Ernie were Carter's *chosen* brothers. They were all jerks – big, fathead jerks.

"Clearly, I am trying to get him to go into the pet store."

"Need some help?"

"No," Caden said quickly. Not from Juan. The cat

laid down and started rolling in the wet slush. Caden breathed out heavily. "You might be helpful."

"Why don't I pick him up? You don't want to squish Huckleberry." Juan took the cat's leash, then bent and hauled the beast into his arms. "Damn. He's a big one, huh? I didn't really see you getting another pet."

"He's a gift." Caden walked quickly toward the store. He could deal with Juan for ten minutes, surely.

"Seriously? Who are you giving him to? Oh, wait. Is it that omega Elijah was talking about? He said you were courting him," Juan said. The cashier stared at Juan's green mohawk, fascinated.

"Yes. He's for Yeo." Caden quickly looked for the basics. He bought the most expensive litter, figuring it had to be the best, but the variety of cat food had him stumped. Grain free? In-door maintenance?"

"Wow, that's a lot of food." Juan pushed a buggy full of cat. "I think Elijah buys Boo this brand."

He pointed to one of the mid-range priced dry foods.

Caden put a huge bag of it in his cart. If it was good enough for Boo, it would likely be good enough for Yeo's cat. He started looking over the pet beds.

"Why don't you like me and Ray?"

Juan's question startled Caden. "What? I don't hate you."

"I didn't say you hated us. You're polite, and you talk to us when you have to. Cain was the same way for a few weeks, then settled in. You never have."

"I don't dislike you." Caden shrugged. "I'm just a distant person."

"You aren't distant to your omega harem."

Caden shot him a look. "Are you saying you want to be part of my harem? That's a bit odd."

"That's not what I'm saying," Juan said, rolling his eyes. He would fit right in with Justin, Grey, and Abel. "It's just strange. We're Carter's best friends, so you would think… Oh. *Oh.*"

"What?" Caden saw the perfect royal blue dog bed. It was perfect for an extra-large cat.

"You're jealous."

Caden dropped the bed and turned around. "What are you talking about? I'm not jealous."

"You are so jealous." Juan sounded amazed. "Fuck, that explains so much."

"You're wrong." Caden grabbed the bed and hurriedly picked out some toys.

"It also explains why Carter turns green anytime someone mentions Grey, Abel, or Justin."

"What does that mean?"

"You aren't the only jealous Benson in town," Juan said with a grin.

He helped Caden load his car and stuffed the poor cat back into its carrier. Caden ignored his stupid grin and sped off without saying goodbye. The idiot didn't know what he was talking about.

Caden parked at the back of the bookstore. The buildings on the street all had living spaces above them, so there were covered parking spaces behind them. Zoe carried a bag of groceries in one hand as she walked up the steps to her apartment over the bakery.

She grinned when she saw him unloading the cat carrier.

"Good luck," she said, shaking her head and opening her door.

It was seven in the evening, so Yeo should be home now. Caden somehow managed to get Sassy, Huckleberry, and the cat up the back stairs and to the spacious balcony attached to Yeo's building. The front door to the apartment was painted blue, making Caden smile. He knocked and waited.

Summer opened the door, grinning when she saw him. "Well, now," she said. "Yeo! Your boyfriend's here."

"What are you talking about?" Yeo came to stand behind her. He blushed, then looked down at his outfit. His omega was usually impeccably dressed. Now he wore plain grey yoga pants, pink unicorn socks, and a pink, long-sleeved shirt covered with narwhals. Cute, black-framed glasses perched on his nose. He hissed at his sister, "Summer, why didn't you say,"

"You look beautiful," Caden said, meaning every single word. His angel was adorable.

"Come on in," Summer said, her southern drawl slipping out. "It's cold out there."

"I brought you a gift, Yeo," he said.

"Two in one day? You wild man, you," Yeo said, eyes teasing. He looked at the cat carrier. "What on earth is that?"

Summer wasn't the only one with a southern drawl.

"He's a Maine Coon cat," Caden said. "You mentioned wanting a pet one day."

Yeo squealed and picked up the carrier. "He's so heavy."

He carried him into his home, and Caden followed behind him with Sassy and Huckleberry.

"Cay Cay," Linc said, walking to him. He held his arms up. "Up."

Caden didn't even try to resist. He picked the little boy up and was rewarded with a sloppy kiss on his cheek.

"Aren't you just the cutest thing in the whole world," Yeo said, cooing at the big cat as he slowly crawled out of the carrier and looked around. "You're just a gorgeous boy."

"I think you broke him," Summer said, laughter in her voice. "Good god, look at him."

Yeo sat on the floor, lap full of cat. "Who's my pretty boy? Who?"

"Yep. He's broken," Summer said. "Come on. I'll show you around."

Caden loved their home. His cabin was big and fancy, but this place was a home. It was colorful, warm, and welcoming. Summer showed him the bedrooms, then knocked on one of the walls in the hall. "There's a bunch of nothing on the other side of the wall here. Yeo says he may use the space in the future, but we were in a hurry when we renovated the place."

"Magnolia is the best gift in the whole world," Yeo said, surprising Caden with a hug. His face was pressed against Huckleberry, but he didn't seem to mind.

Caden sure as hell didn't mind. His omega was in his arms. Linc patted his papa's head and giggled. Yeo lifted his face and pressed his lips to Caden's. The world faded away until Yeo's taste was the only thing that existed. It ended too soon. Linc pressed kiss after kiss on Caden and Yeo's cheeks. Giggling between each one. Yeo pulled a few rabbit hairs off his lips, eyes watching Caden shyly.

"Wow," Summer said. "That was seriously the least romantic first kiss I've ever seen. Not great timing, bro."

Caden shook his head. "It was perfect."

Yeo watched Amy Pettit smile as she suggested a new author to a regular customer. *Holy shit*, Yeo thought. He had regular customers. After a month, The Book Worm still had a steady flow of daily customers. The book clubs were doing well, and the children story times were becoming more and more popular. Amy was a lifesaver.

Yeo was able to focus more on bookkeeping, ordering inventory, the online site, and marketing. He wanted to hire even more people, so he could keep the store open longer. The town would like that, and it would make longer summer days more profitable. He hoped he would be able to maintain his numbers when summer rolled around. With more things to do, business might droop.

"What are you doing over here?" Bennett's voice was directly behind him and startled the crap out of him.

"Bennett!" Yeo loved his best friend. He hugged the man even though he had seen him every day since the day they'd met. He pulled back. "I'm arranging some romance novels in the window displays."

He looked around the store. It was decorated for Valentine's Day in pink, red, and white.

"Good idea," Bennett said, picking up some books and helping him. "Where's Linc? I want some story time."

"My sweet, darling boy is upstairs so I don't yell at him again. He was playing in Magnolia's litterbox when I woke up this morning. Naked."

Bennett laughed. "How did he get in the laundry room?"

"He went under the baby gate," Yeo said. "I left it off the ground so Magnolia could scoot under it. Linc can scoot too."

"Who's watching him?"

"Caden. He brought his laptop and is working while he keeps an eye on Linc." Yeo pressed his lips together, thinking about Caden's kiss that morning. They had perfected kissing over the last month. Maybe they could work on perfecting something else on their Valentine's Day date.

They just needed to arrange to have that date.

"Caden is upstairs, watching Linc," Bennett repeated. He smiled. "Has he asked you on an actual date yet?"

"No," Yeo said, sighing. "He brings me gifts every night and has dinner with Summer and me. He helps her with her homework, then gives Linc his bath and reads him to sleep."

"He fits, huh?"

"Perfectly," Yeo said. "After Summer goes to bed, we sit on the couch and talk, then kiss, then talk some more, then kiss and kiss. I can't stand it when he leaves."

Bennett shook his head. "Still no date though. I think you're going to have to take the next step. Caden has done well with courting, but maybe you need to be the one to push for more."

"What if he doesn't want more? What if he doesn't want to date me?" Yeo thought about it. "What if he doesn't want us to be a public thing?"

Bennett snorted. "That is the stupidest thing I've ever heard. Your whole relationship has been public from the start. Everyone in town knows Caden Benson is crazy about you."

"Mr. Yeo Cook?"

Yeo turned around. A woman stood next to them. She wore slacks, a thick sweater, and a colorful scarf. Yeo didn't know her at all.

"Yes. That's me."

She pushed her glasses up her nose. "My name is Dana Butler. I work for Social Services." She handed him a card. It had her name and contact information on it. "My supervisor's name and contact information are on the back."

"May I help you?" Yeo had no idea what she could possibly need from him.

"There have been some allegations made against

you involving environmental neglect concerning your son and your sister." Yeo's mouth dropped open. Ms. Butler looked around. "I would like to wait here for a police escort, but I have a court order to inspect your home. The police department is sending someone now."

"What exact allegations have been made?" Bennett sounded furious.

"And you are?" The woman seemed genuinely curious.

"Bennett Wilson. I'm Yeo's best friend."

"It's nice to meet you." She looked back at Yeo. "The exact allegations claim that your living space is unsuitable for anyone to live in, much less two children. These pictures were sent to us along with the claim."

She handed him some pictures. He flipped through them carefully. The upstairs had been one empty, rotting, open space.

"These were taken before I renovated the building. We weren't living here at the time."

"I suspected as much," she said, pushing her glasses up her nose again. "We take every claim seriously, Mr. Cook. The sooner I can verify that these pictures are inaccurate, the better."

"Ms. Butler?" Tanner Jones looked pissed. The police officer quickly approached. "This is stupid. I've been upstairs myself. These pictures are out of date."

"I understand, officer, but we must be certain," she said firmly. "Mr. Cook, would you please come with us? You don't have to, but it might reassure you."

"Yes," Yeo said. "Um, let me tell Amy."

Bennett followed on his heels. As his belly got bigger, Yeo's friend got slower. "What the fuck is going on? Your apartment is gorgeous. I'm coming with to keep an eye on her."

"Amy, I have an emergency to deal with. I'll be back as soon as I can," Yeo said. His voice trembled, and he hated it. He didn't have anything to hide, but he loved Summer and Linc more than anything in the world. The idea of losing them made him want to hide in his room and cry.

"Sure thing," she said, worried. "Anything I can help with?"

"No, but thank you." He walked back to Tanner and Ms. Butler. "I'm ready if you'll follow me. We can use the interior entrance if you'd like."

"You have two entrances?"

"Yes. One right here," he said, gesturing to the locked door at the back of the store. He unlocked it, and they started up the steps. "The other is at the back of the store. Each of the buildings on this street have upstairs living space, so they all have a back entrance. It's a nice neighborhood."

He told himself not to ramble. Less information was better.

She took notes as they walked. They reached the door, and he unlocked it, walking in.

"Papa!" Linc poked his head around the couch. He held his stuffed rabbit in his arms. Huckleberry hopped beside him as he slowly headed toward Yeo.

Caden looked over from his spot on the couch. His laptop sat on the coffee table. "Yeo? What's wrong?"

"Social Services has a court order to look over the apartment," he said, voice breaking at the end. Caden jumped up and ran over.

"May I see it? What are the allegations?" He stared Ms. Butler down. She simply handed him the pictures and walked around the room, taking notes.

Yeo bent to pick up Linc and told Caden what she had said. "Someone sent them out-of-date pictures. Why would they do that?"

"To cause trouble," Caden said, voice hard.

"You have nothing to worry about," Bennett said. "Your home is just fine, and you take good care of your kids."

"I'm going into the bedrooms now, alright?" Ms. Butler stood in the kitchen. Sassy sat at the woman's feet, panting happily as she followed the stranger around.

Yeo rushed over. "Okay. Yeah." He followed her as she looked at Summer's room first. His sister wasn't exactly a neat freak, but he did make her pick up her room once a week. Luckily, it wasn't too bad.

"This is Summer's room?"

"Yes," he said, managing not say anything else.

Ms. Butler took notes, nodded, then went to Linc's room. Yeo's son had a ton of toys, but they weren't strewn about the room. Today. His bed wasn't made, but the sheets were clean. "He just started sleeping in a big boy bed a couple of months ago,"

Bennett pressed his hand to Yeo's back, and the warmth seeped into his cold body.

The woman again took notes, then went to his room. The master bedroom was brightly decorated and relatively neat. Yeo had a new desk pressed against the window overlooking the streets, a gift from Bennett. His bed was huge and unmade. He had an ottoman at the end, and Magnolia stretched out across it, sleeping peacefully. She looked over his bathroom, then went back into the living room.

"Alright. That should do it," she said. She watched Yeo, face grave. "Obviously, these allegations were false. I'll speak with my supervisor, Mr. Cook, and you shouldn't hear from us again. I am sorry for the trouble."

"It's okay," he said, voice full of relief. "You have to do your job."

"Yes," she said. "I'll show myself out."

She turned and quickly left, making sure Sassy was inside the apartment before she shut the door.

"Oh, my god," Yeo said, wailing. He clutched Linc to him and cried into his son's silky hair. Caden's arms were around him in seconds.

"It's okay, angel. The woman had to treat this like any other investigation. You're fine," Caden said.

"Who sent those pictures?" Bennett looked over his phone. "I took pictures of them, but they just look like pictures."

"CPS isn't allowed to reveal who made the allegations," Caden said. He shook his head. "Let me talk to a few people."

"Anyone who lives in town would know this place was renovated," Tanner said. He ran his hands through his hair. "Why would they want to do that to Yeo?"

Yeo grabbed his cell and thumbed through his contacts. "It might not be someone from town." He hit speaker phone.

"Yeo," Richard Cook said. Even over the phone, Yeo's grandpa's deep voice made Yeo swallow.

"Grandpa. I just had a little visit from CPS."

"Oh. How unfortunate. Someone else will take in the children I'm sure. You're welcome back in the business of course. As long as Summer isn't with you, your father would be glad to have you back."

"My children weren't taken," Yeo said angrily. "What the hell?"

"You're living in a dump, and they let you keep the children? That's preposterous," Richard said.

"I'm so sorry, grandpa, but your pictures were out of date." Yeo's voice rose until he was yelling. "What the hell were you trying to do?"

"I have no idea what you're talking about. I have to go." The man hung up on him.

"He either sent the pictures or knows who did," Yeo said, snarling. Linc hid his face against his neck.

"Papa?"

Yeo calmed himself and kissed the little boy's cheek. "It's okay, baby. Papa just needed to yell a little."

"He wants you back in Cook Enterprises," Caden said thoughtfully. "If he's willing to stoop this low, I wonder what else he'll do." He kissed Yeo gently. "I'll look into things, angel. Try not to worry."

"We'll figure this out, Yeo," Bennett said.

"Cook Enterprises is that big company in Nashville, right?" Tanner sounded thoughtful. "Watch your business, man. If they want you back, they may try some shit."

YEO STRADDLED Caden on the couch later that night. He needed his alpha so badly. Their kisses were slow and hot, warming Yeo's body. Caden's fingers dug into Yeo's hips, pulling their bodies together, and Yeo gasped at the feel of Caden's hard erection through his pants.

"Caden, I need you," he said. "Please?"

"Are you sure?"

"Positive," Yeo said.

He laughed when Caden stood, holding Yeo to him. He wrapped his legs around his alpha's waist.

"Caden. I should tell you something." He cupped his alpha's beautiful face in his hands. "I haven't been with a man before. I'm gay, always have been, but I've never been with a man. I've only had sex once, and it was horrible."

"With your ex-wife?"

"Yeah."

Caden kissed him. "This will be better, angel. I'll make sure of it."

Yeo laughed softly. "Of course, it will. You'll be there. I just don't want you to be disappointed if I mess something up."

"I won't be disappointed, Yeo." Caden set him gently on the bed. He kissed Yeo, tongue entwining with his. His alpha ran his hands up Yeo's sides, pulling his shirt with him. He pulled it over Yeo's head, then his lips were on Yeo's nipples, licking and sucking.

"Damn," Yeo said, arching up. "Caden!"

Caden's mouth moved on. He placed small kisses on Yeo's soft stomach, and Yeo's body clenched. He wanted Caden inside him.

"Please. Inside me?"

"Condoms," Caden asked, digging around in Yeo's bedside table for lube. He tossed it on the bed, then started pulling Yeo's pants down his legs. His cock popped up, happy to see his alpha. "Do you have any, angel?"

"No condoms," Yeo said. "Please."

Caden met his eyes. "Yeo? You could get pregnant."

"Good. I told you I have baby fever. If it happens, I'll be the happiest omega in the world. Please, Caden."

Yeo didn't recognize the look in Caden's eyes. It looked like a mixture of hunger and joy and something else. Caden's tongue traced around Yeo's pucker.

"Caden!" Yeo gasped, dick so hard he thought it might explode. A finger entered him as Caden's mouth covered the tip of Yeo's dick. "Oh my god, oh my god," Yeo said. "Caden."

Another finger stretched him, and Caden licked a path from the base of his cock to the tip. A third finger was added before Caden slowly slid his cock inside Yeo.

Yeo pulled his alpha into a kiss, gasping at the

taste of himself on Caden's lips. He kissed him as Caden rocked against him. A few moments later, his body heated and shuddered as Caden's hot cum filled him. He shot his own release against his alpha's stomach.

"Yeo?" Caden panted, body entangled with his own. "I love you, Yeo. I know it's soon, but I want you to know. I'm yours."

Yeo nuzzled his alpha's neck, before meeting Caden's serious brown eyes. "I've never loved anyone like this, Caden. I love Summer, my son, and my papa, but I've never loved anyone like I love you." He laughed even as his eyes grew wet. "This feeling is crazy, isn't it? It's like fear, joy, excitement, and lust all in one. I adore you, Caden. You make me want to quote fucking Shakespeare."

Caden laughed, holding Yeo's body close to his. "I know what you mean. Grey and the others would never let me live it down. I'm supposed to be stoic and quiet."

"You talk all the time," Yeo said, confused.

"To you," Caden said. "To be fair, I've opened up a lot with Grey, Justin, and Abel, but you're different. You're my omega. I can say whatever I want when we have our nightly talks."

"Hmm," Yeo said, hiding his pleasure. He loved their talks. "You still haven't told me what you do for a living."

Caden groaned, hiding his face. "Soon."

"'Soon' he says." Yeo hmphed. "Now that we're in love, will you go on a date with me? Valentine's Day is

Friday. I've never had a romantic Valentine's Day. It's always just been another day."

"I thought we were already dating," Caden said, eyes wide. "Dinner and kissing wasn't dating?"

Yeo stroked Caden's hair from his forehead. "I thought you didn't want to be seen with me in public."

Caden snorted. "Are you crazy?"

"Oh my god, you just snorted. Caden Benson just snorted," Yeo said, voice exaggerated with shock. He broke into giggles when Caden started tickling him.

"Our Valentine's Day date will be perfect," his alpha said.

# CHAPTER 7

*C*aden had fought for clients in court hundreds of time. He'd faced old-school, grumpy judges with a stoic expression. He'd dodged shady questions with eloquence and skill.

Now, standing on his omega's doorstep, he was nervous, sweating, and scared to death. He clutched the rose bush in his arm. Janelle had insisted that cut roses were horrible and pushed the red, climbing rose on him. He took a deep breath and knocked on Yeo's door. Their reservations were at seven, and he hoped Yeo didn't mind the longer drive to get to the nice restaurant.

The door opened, and Caden's eyes widened. Yeo looked terrible. He was flushed, and his nose was bright red. He had a wad of tissue stuck up each nostril, and his eyes were red from crying. Tears still streamed down his face. He was dressed in his favorite narwhal pajamas and thick wool socks.

"I'm sick," he wailed. "I don't want to miss our date,

but I have a fever, and my nose is pouring snot all over everything."

Caden pulled the messy, damp man into his arms. "It's okay, angel. No one said we had to go out for Valentine's Day. I'll take care of you, okay? Where are Summer and Linc?"

"I sent them to Bennett's house, so they won't get sick," Yeo said. Magnolia threaded between their feet, purring loudly. Caden's omega started crying harder. "I miss my babies."

"Come on. Let's get you set up on the couch." He felt Yeo's head, and he was warm. What the hell was he supposed to do? He had never taken care of someone before. He set him on the couch and quickly gathered all the used tissues off the coffee table. "I'll be right back."

He dumped the tissues in the garbage and gagged as one stuck to his hand. He washed his hands at the sink, twice, then called his mother.

"Caden, dear. How nice to hear from you," Susan said.

"Yeo is sick. He has a fever, and his nose is full of snot. What do I do?" Caden tried to contain his panic. His mother didn't have to know how incompetent he was.

"Oh, no. Is it a cold or the flu?"

"Uh, I don't know. Hold on." He looked over at the couch at his pitiful omega. "Do you have a cold or the flu?"

"I have hell in my nose, Caden. Hell." Yeo stuffed fresh tissues up his nose.

Susan laughed in his ear. "Oh, my. That poor boy sounds like he'll be a handful." She listed out what medicine to get him and directions on how to make him feel a little better. "Keep him hydrated and try to get some soup in him. Good luck, baby. Your dad and I are looking forward to meeting your omega when we make the move. Have a good night."

He set his phone on the counter, then went to the master bath and started running the water. He dug through Yeo's medicine cabinets and found some Tylenol. "Angel? How about a hot bath? It'll help with your congestion."

Yeo whimpered. "I have to move?"

Caden handed him a glass of water and the medicine.

"I'll carry you," he said. He waited until Yeo swallowed, then scooped him up and carried him to the bathroom.

"I love you," Yeo said, laying his head on his shoulder. "Why do you have to go home all the time? I miss Sassy and Huckleberry too. Why can't you all just stay with us?"

Caden stood him on his feet and quickly undressed his omega. He tried to ignore looking, but he couldn't help himself. He noticed Yeo's omega line was pink and a little swollen. He'd obviously been scratching at it. Caden grinned slowly. Damn.

"I'll spend some more time here, alright? Now get in the tub. You relax, and I'm going to go make you some soup. Here's some washrags. Put them on your chest."

"I wish my papa were here," Yeo said. "I'm such a

baby when I'm sick. I bet he'd be like you and take good care of me."

Caden sat on the closed toilet. "You never told me about your omega father. How did he meet your dad?"

"I have no idea," Yeo said. "They didn't run in the same social circles and have absolutely nothing in common. I'm always surprised when I think about my dad even being with an omega. Grandpa has always been adamant that omegas have no place in society. They just pretend I'm a beta."

"They did meet though."

"Yeah," Yeo said, sinking into the warm water. He pulled the tissue out of his nose and tossed it toward the garbage can. He put a wet rag over his face and sighed. "Papa's family is super traditional and conservative. His dad is a Christian preacher, and he thinks omegas do have a place in society. One place. Women and omegas are meant to be married, pregnant, and stay-at-home parents. They are to submit to their partner no matter what."

"That doesn't sound any better than your alpha father," Caden said.

"Nope," Yeo said. "He'd already arranged a marriage for my papa too. When I happened, they were pissed. At first, they'd tried to get him to abort."

"I thought you said he was a Christian preacher?"

"Yeah. Apparently, he is also a hypocrite. Go figure," Yeo said, shrugging. "Papa refused. The second I was born, his parents handed me over to my dad and stepmom. Papa wasn't supposed to ever have any contact with me. His arranged marriage went through, but my stepmom, Fawn, stayed in contact with him and told him all about me. He started calling from a burner phone on my birthdays and every holiday. I never knew when he would call, but he always did."

"You said he missed your last birthday," Caden said.

Tears filled Yeo's eyes, and he sniffled. "I had to change my number when I left Tennessee, because the company paid for my phone. Fawn said she would give Papa my new number, but she said he never called."

"That doesn't sound right," Caden said. Especially not considering all the crap Yeo's grandfather had tried to pull.

"I don't know," Yeo said sadly. "Maybe he's tired of me. All I do is talk about myself during our calls. I know he has more kids now. There are four of them." He splashed and watched the water drops fall. "He never talks about himself or my siblings."

"Hmm, try not to worry, angel," Caden said. He stood and headed for the door. "Relax here, and I'll make you some Valentine's Day soup."

He smiled when Yeo laughed.

He left his omega in the bath with Magnolia sprawled on the bathroom rug keeping an eye on their man. He started digging through the refrigerator and pulled out all the vegetables he could find. He scowled and made a call, leaving a message with his private investigator as he chopped vegetables. He'd figure everything out for his love. He'd make everything better.

~

CADEN WOKE to Yeo's loud snores. He held his omega in his arms and nuzzled the top of his head. Their Valentine's Day date had been messy, disgusting, and completely unromantic. Caden grinned. It had been perfect. He'd learned more about Yeo and had gotten to spend some time with him. Dirty tissues were disgusting, but his angel was worth it. He was worth anything. Caden remembered Yeo's omega line and wondered. Yes, it had been a great night.

He slipped out of bed and started cleaning the house. Magnolia watched him from the couch, completely unhelpful. *He gets along well with Sassy and Huckleberry,* he mused.

There was that little patch of yard at the back of the building. Right now, it was covered with snow, but soon enough, it would be grass. They could fence it in. Next door, Zoe had her little patch fenced in with wrought iron. It looked good.

He really didn't have many things of his own, he realized as he started wiping everything down with Clorox wipes. He could keep the cabin as a weekend place or sell it. It didn't matter to him at all. Summer had said there was empty space left to renovate if they had more kids. Hmm, he would need some storage for his zombie apocalypse stash. Just in case. Now that he thought of it, if society ended, they would need a place to retreat to, so he needed to keep the cabin.

He put a load of clothes in the washer, then fed and watered Magnolia. He checked the rose bush and put a little water into it too. Yeo still slept, so Caden ran downstairs to check on the bookstore.

Amy had already opened but seemed relieved to see him. "Yeo was supposed to come in this morning. Is he okay?"

"He has a nasty cold," Caden said. "He needs to rest up today, but I can help out. Will you show me how to use the register?"

"Sure," she said and walked him through everything. She watched him with a couple customers, then declared him ready. "If you'll spot me a few times during the day, we'll do fine."

"No problem. I'll grab you a coffee, then go check on Yeo." Caden left her and stood in line at Honey Buns.

Zoe leaned on the counter, watching him with a smirk. "So, how did your super romantic, hot, and sexy Valentine's Day date go?"

"Perfectly," Caden said, smiling widely.

Zoe blinked. "What the fuck? You're smiling."

"Yeo makes me happy," he said. "By the way, who did your fence in the back? I was thinking of having ours done for Sassy."

"Ours? Oh, this is just so yummy," she said. "I can't wait to call Elijah and let him know that super stoic Caden is grinning and happy and planning the future."

He raised a brow.

"Don't raise that brow at me," she said and handed him his order. "One perfect date and you're moving in. That's prime gold information, there."

He left her, dropped Amy's coffee off at the register, then went back upstairs. Yeo was exactly where he'd left him. Magnolia lay beside him, offering him a little more warmth. *Good cat*, he thought. He wished he had brought his laptop so he could get some writing done, but he hadn't. It really would make life easier if he moved in.

A few hours later, a groggy Yeo stumbled out of the bedroom. "Caden? Can I have more soup?" He plopped down on the couch next to him and settled his head on Caden's shoulder. "I even brushed my teeth, so I wouldn't chase you away."

Caden laughed. "I don't want to go anywhere if you aren't there."

"I remember what I said last night," Yeo said. His large, black eyes watched Caden. "Would you move in with us? I haven't even seen your cabin, so you may not want to."

"It's a nice place, but it doesn't have you and the kids," Caden said. "I'd love to move in. In fact, as soon as you're feeling better, I'll go pack my things. I don't really have a lot. Just books, clothes, and my computer."

"Are you ever going to tell me what your job is? If you're moving in, I should know. Right?"

Caden grinned. He knew Yeo would accept him as a romance writer, but he liked keeping it secret. "I'll tell you soon enough."

Yeo snorted, kind of. Snorting with a cold was difficult, and he started coughing. "You're a tease, Caden Benson. A tease!"

# CHAPTER 8

$\mathcal{Y}$eo sat on the bed and petted Magnolia while Caden added his clothes to their closet. He still felt sucky, but he was getting better. Amy had watched the store for the past two days by herself. He really needed a couple more people. Sassy hopped up on the bed and lay down next to him. He scratched her silky ears and smiled.

"I need to hire more people, don't I?" He hugged Magnolia and sighed. He missed his babies. He couldn't wait until Summer and Linc came home. Bennett had talked him into leaving them with him for one more night. That man really needed ten more babies to keep him occupied.

"Are you alright with my bookshelves?" Caden sounded uncertain, and Yeo didn't like it.

"Anywhere you want. This is your home too." He looked at them from the bed. Caden had placed one on each side of the large window above the desk. "They look really good there." He scratched his stomach. The damn thing had been itchy for a few days now. He really needed to change his moisturizer. "Your desk is bigger than mine too."

They'd put his desk down in his office. Yeo felt bad, but he didn't want to share his desk. Bennett gave it to him.

"I just don't want to take over. This is a big step for us."

"It is," Yeo agreed. "I'm ready though."

Caden smiled wide. "I am too."

Pounding on their door startled Yeo. Sassy started barking and ran into the living room. Caden frowned and followed. Yeo yawned and made himself get out of the bed. He passed Huckleberry in the hallway. The rabbit slept in one of the many pet beds spread throughout the apartment.

Yeo stared at Ray. The man stood in the door and was angry. Really angry. Yeo had never seen the gentle beta do anything more than growl playfully when he pretended to steal Linc's tater tots.

"What is wrong with you? Am I not good enough? I can't believe you've been doing this behind my back!" Ray poked his finger into Caden's chest after each statement.

What the hell? Caden would never cheat on him. Would he?

"I didn't think you'd feel this way," Caden said. "I didn't want to bother you, and he was available."

"Excuse me?" Yeo stomped his foot. "I was available? You said you loved me, Caden."

The two men looked at him like he was crazy.

"I do love you, angel," Caden said.

Ray winced. "I didn't think about how that sounded, Yeo. I'm sorry." He pointed at Caden with a glare. "This jerk went behind my back to use a different investigator from the company I work at. *I'm* the Wilsons and Bensons' investigator, not Walter Douglas."

Yeo rolled his eyes. "You two are ridiculous."

He went to the kitchen to make himself a sandwich. He listened as the two men argued.

"Here's the information Walter gathered," Ray said, tossing a file on the coffee table. "He said you had another job for him?"

"Fine," Caden said. "I can't believe you're so upset over this."

They sat at the couch. One man on each end.

"I'm the investigator the Wilsons and Bensons use," Ray say stubbornly. "It's what I do, damn it. What's the second job?"

"I want you to find information on Yeo's papa. He's an omega named Dean Wagner. He lives in Jackson, Tennessee," Caden said. "His alpha's name is Simon Wagner."

Yeo squealed and ran to his alpha, climbing into his lap. "I didn't even think of hiring someone to find him. You're a genius, baby."

He kissed his cheek and snuggled in, taking another bite of his sandwich.

"I'll let you know what I find," Ray said, eyes softening as he watched Yeo. "Walt found a few things of interest about Richard Cook. He's blacklisted Yeo at all of the financing companies that he has influence with. He's also been very verbal in his displeasure with Yeo. He tells everyone that he cruelly divorced Tracy and stole her child, leaving her alone and destitute. He hasn't mentioned Summer at all."

Yeo snorted. "I don't need financing. I'm no Elijah, but I've made some smart investments. I'm also not starting another Fortune 500 company. I bought this building with cash, and as long as it stays in the black, I'll be okay."

Ray shrugged. "From what Walt could tell, the man has done everything he can think of to prevent you from being successful. The problem is that you don't seem to measure success like him. You have a bookstore in a small town. There's not much he can do about that in Tennessee."

"Good news," Caden said.

"Yeah. Unfortunately, Walt found some bad news too. A custody suit has been filed for Lincoln Cook."

"What? That's not possible," Yeo said. First CPS and now this? He should be worried, but he was just angry.

"Your ex-wife filed the necessary forms in Nashville Friday morning," Ray said.

"She has no possible chance of winning. What is she after?" Yeo was genuinely baffled. What could Tracy want? Caden's body was stiff beneath him, and his face was frozen.

"Courts often give preference to the mother, angel. We need to prepare to fight this. Why didn't she pursue custody before?"

Yeo stood and grabbed his phone. He set his smart

phone to record and dialed Tracy's number by memory. He put the call on speakerphone and set it on the table.

"Yeo," she answered after one ring. "Have you finally come to your senses? Are you coming home?"

"What the hell kind of game are you playing, Tracy?" He didn't hide the anger in his voice.

"You've already heard about the custody suit? I'm surprised," she said, pleased.

"You have zero chance of winning, Tracy. What are you after?"

"I'm a distraught mother," she said, laughing. "Why wouldn't I have a chance?"

"He's not yours, you idiot. I was artificially inseminated. Have you forgotten that? You didn't give birth to him. You didn't financially or emotionally support him. You didn't even legally adopt him. You have no right to him," Yeo said. "We even signed a contract saying that when I got pregnant. You didn't want to be bound to him in any way. Remember?"

"No one but you and I know that," she hissed. "You wouldn't possibly let Richard or Michael know you gave birth."

Yeo's body shook with anger, and he was literally speechless. He stalked into his bedroom, hearing Caden take over the call.

"Hi, Mrs. Cook," Caden said. "I'm Mr. Cook's lawyer, and I can assure you he has no problem providing that information to a court, jury, or the media."

Yeo grabbed what he needed and brought it to

Caden, tearing open the envelope and showing him the pictures.

"Thank you, Yeo. Mrs. Cook, it looks like you were unfaithful during the marriage," Caden said. "I see evidence of seven different men." He looked at Yeo's note. "Including Michael and Richard Cook. Oh, that won't look good in court at all."

"You wouldn't dare make that public, Yeo," she said, screeching. "Your father would kill you."

"My son," he bit out. "You are trying to take my son from me. Try me, Tracy. Just you fucking try me."

"Why did you even have him?" She sounded as pissed as Yeo felt. "We were fine. Everything was fine. You had the company; I had money and men. Why did you have to bring that omega brat into the world? Nothing has gone right since then."

Caden took one look at Yeo's face and spoke quickly. "Tracy, I encourage you to reconsider your suit immediately. We will gladly meet you in court, but all of this information will become public knowledge. I promise you that."

"Fine," she spat out. "I told Richard it wouldn't work anyway. A gentleman wouldn't air a lady's dirty laundry, but you aren't a gentleman, are you, Yeo?"

"I'm sorry," Ray said, shaking his head. "Is she for real? She honestly thinks that the right thing to do here is to let her have your son—who she hates—after she fucked your father and grandfather? Seriously?"

"How dare you," she said, voice high and annoying. "I could have taken him for everything he had when we divorced, but I was kind."

"We signed prenups," Yeo corrected her. "I was *kind* and gave her more than I was required to."

"Again, drop the suit, Mrs. Cook. If not, we'll see you in court." Caden ended the call, then looked at Yeo, eyes wide. "Holy shit, angel. Your ex is crazy."

"That is some *Dynasty* type shit right there," Ray said, pointing to the pictures spread across the table.

"Tracy isn't crazy, just self-absorbed," he said. "She wouldn't have tried that on her own though. Grandpa and Dad are probably pushing her."

"She said Richard, not Michael and Richard," Ray said. "According to Walt's report, your father has been hush-hush about the whole situation with you, your divorce, and Summer."

"They want you back in the company," Caden said. "That was the point behind reporting you to CPS. He can't touch your business, so he is taking this route."

"Will she drop the suit?" Ray asked.

"Yeah," Yeo said. "She is all about her image. If this information got out, she would have to leave the state. That's not something she wants to do. Her family has a lot of standing in Nashville. Not so much anywhere else."

Ray stood. "I'm going to keep looking into this. I'll see if we can find some leverage against them. I'll find your papa too, Yeo."

He nodded, then left.

Yeo sat back in Caden's lap. "Why can't they just let us be happy? They don't want Summer. They don't want me—at least, not the real me. Why can't we just be free?"

He rubbed his face against Caden's chest.

"I don't know, angel. I feel bad saying this right now, but I'm really happy to have my parents. We both did the same stupid thing. We tried to make ourselves what our parents wanted. Mother and Father have been wonderful about accepting and supporting me now. I wish you had that from your dad," Caden said.

Yeo sighed. His dad would never accept him for what he was. He was an omega, and that one fact kept him from standing a chance with Michael Cook.

"He will never love me," Yeo said. "But that's okay. I love myself."

"Damn, you are one amazing man," Caden said. "Not too many people can do that. Trust me, I know."

They sat together for hours, wrapped up in one another. Yeo focused on Caden's breathing and his steady heartbeat. He slowly grew calmer, his mind clearing. He had his alpha, his son, and his sister. He had his best friend and a ton of other friends. He had Magnolia, Sassy, and Huckleberry. He had a damn good life, and no one would take that from him.

# CHAPTER 9

"You should tell him about Roxanne," Zoe said, sitting at the booth with Caden. "You're a wonderful man, Caden, and Yeo is crazy about you. Hell, you've been together for just over a month, and you're already living with him. That should tell you something."

"I will," Caden said. "I'm not worried about how he'll react. I'm just torturing him now. He keeps guessing weird things. This morning he asked me if I worked for the mafia."

Zoe laughed. "Here I thought you were doubting yourself. That poor omega."

"Caden," Elijah said, sliding into the seat behind him. His belly was getting bigger and bigger each day. "I have news for you. There's going to be an ambush this afternoon."

"What are you talking about?"

"Ray, Ernie, and Juan talked and decided that you need to work things out with Carter. They're going to kidnap him, then ambush you to make sure you guys talk it out," Elijah said. "I didn't even know you two were having problems. Why didn't I know this?"

Caden sighed. "Drama. So much drama."

"I just texted Grey. If Carter is going to have his besties, it's only fair you have your Hot Mess Club," Zoe said. She glared at him. "I can't believe you guys didn't let me in your club."

"Zo Zo," Elijah said. "You're mine. I'm your posse."

"You're the best posse ever," Zoe said, blowing Elijah kisses. "Do I need to be there to support Carter?"

"Zoe," Caden said. "You're *my* neighbor. Don't you have any loyalty?"

"Neighbor?" Elijah eyes narrowed. Shit. Caden had forgotten to tell anyone about the move. "You're living with Yeo? You didn't tell us that you moved in with your omega?" He stood and glared at Caden. "It's on now, Caden. You've been warned. We're bringing the love tonight, Zo Zo. Be there." He stalked off.

"Where?" Zoe called after him. "Where am I supposed to be? Damn it."

"Considering I'll either be in the bookstore or at home, it shouldn't be too hard to figure it out," Caden said dryly. "I thought you were all set to spread the news about the move?"

Zoe sighed. "I was being nice. It hurt, but I wanted to try. I'll never do it again." She gave him a look. "Why didn't you tell anyone you moved?"

"It's only been a few days," Caden said. "To be honest, my mind has been on the trouble Yeo's grandfather has been giving him."

"I get that," Zoe said. "I guess, I just thought you'd call Carter to help you move or something."

"Tanner had the day off and came to help," Caden said, shrugging.

Zoe slapped his shoulder. "That right there is the problem. Why did you call Tanner and not Carter?"

Caden thought for a minute. "I don't know. I talk to Tanner more, and I knew he was off that day."

She shook her head. "You deserve the beat down of love you're going to get."

"What is a beat down of love exactly?"

"I have no idea. I need to go strategize with Elijah. We'll need to coordinate outfits too," she said, sliding out of the booth. "I'll get you a latte for Yeo."

"That's alright. I don't think coffee is good for him right now," Caden said without thinking.

Zoe slid back in the booth. "Caden. Sweet, silent, brooding Caden. Tell Ms. Zoe what the fuck you mean by that."

"You can't tell anyone," he said, wincing. "I don't even know if it's what I think it is."

"Did we not just agree that I need to tell everyone everything?"

"Yeo doesn't even realize it yet. His omega line is swollen and pink. It itches like crazy," Caden said.

Zoe vibrated in her seat, trying not to squeal. "Is he pregnant? I know he wants another baby, so this would be so awesome!"

"I think he is," Caden said, smiling.

"Oh, look at that smile," Zoe said. "You're really happy about it?"

"I love Linc and Summer," he said. "Why wouldn't I love another baby?"

"You better hope Yeo figures it out soon," Zoe said. "I don't know how long I can sit on this information."

Caden got up. "I have to get going. I need to finish a chapter today to stay on track."

"Don't ignore me, Caden," Zoe said.

He ignored her and went into the bookstore. Yeo was still banished to the apartment. He probably wasn't contagious anymore, but Amy didn't want to take chances. He had given her breaks during the day and closed in the evenings.

"Ms. Amy, do you need anything before I go check on Yeo," Caden asked.

"Nope," she said. "I'll text you if I need a break. Are the kids coming home tonight?"

"Yes. Bennett is bringing Linc by in a few hours. Summer will be home after school." Caden was nervous as hell. They didn't know that he'd moved in. He hoped they didn't mind.

He left Amy and went upstairs. Yeo lay stretched out on the couch watching *Ellen*. His head on a massive pile of pillows, and all three pets were cuddling with him.

"Hey, handsome," Yeo said, smiling at him. "How was your morning? Are you going to get to work?"

Caden grinned. "Yes, I am." He picked up his laptop and sat in one of the armchairs. "I'll just work right here."

"Caden," Yeo wailed. "Tell me!"

"You've looked at my book collection, right?"

"Yes," Yeo said. "You have excellent taste in romance novels."

"I'm a writer," Caden said.

Yeo sat up, dislodging Huckleberry from his chest. "You're a writer? Are you published? Do you have a pen name? You write romance, don't you?"

"I am published. I do write romance. My pen name is…" Caden began, but was interrupted.

"Roxanne Baxter," Yeo said, clapping. "That's why your dad bought all those books."

"Yes," Caden said. "There you have it. My dirty secret."

"Does this mean that I'll get to read your books early?"

"No," Caden said.

Yeo shot him a dirty look. "You said you loved me."

"You can read them when they come out just like everyone else," he said. He got up and kissed Yeo's scowl away. "I do love you, angel."

"Fine," Yeo said, sinking back into the couch. "Will you make something yummy for dinner tonight?"

"Sure. We might get interrupted though. Apparently, my brother's friends think Carter and I have issues, so they're going to try to force us to talk."

"Good, you two circle around each other like two tomcats. It's weird." He made a face. "Not that I'm an expert on family."

Someone pounded on the front door.

"It's a little early for your intervention, isn't it?"

Caden opened the door to find Justin, Grey, Abel, Bennett, and Linc on his doorstep.

"Daddy," Linc called, holding out his arms to Caden.

Everyone stared at the little boy.

"Daddy," he said again. His tone left no doubt that he wanted Caden right that second. Caden took him from Bennett and hugged him tight, tears in his eyes.

"Yeo! Linc called me daddy," Caden said, running to his omega.

"Aww," Yeo said. "Smart boy." He held his arms out. "Did you miss me, baby?"

Linc hugged Caden. "Missed daddy."

"Well," Yeo said, sniffing. "I see how it is."

"He's my boy," Caden said smugly.

"How are you feeling, Yeo?" Bennett sat on the edge of the couch and gave his friend a big hug.

"I'm feeling much better. My jerkhead alpha took good care of me." Yeo glared at Caden. "Then he stole my son."

"Linc knows who his papa is," Bennett said with a laugh. "I'll start on lunch. You boys need to figure out what Caden's going to say to Carter."

"Why do we have to make a plan? Can't Carter and I just talk?" Caden nuzzled Linc's head. Damn, he'd missed him.

"I don't know," Bennett said. "Can you? So far it hasn't happened, and now it's causing trouble among your friends. Carter glared at Grey yesterday. He *glared*, Caden."

"He did," Grey said, nodding.

"What did you do?" Caden asked. Carter would never be mean to an omega. It wasn't in his nature.

"Butterball *may* have stolen his shoe while he was

fixing the kitchen sink. I made him take them off, because I'd just mopped. By the time we found it, Butterball *may* have chewed it up," Grey said. He fixed big, soulful eyes on Caden. "He glared at me, Caden."

Justin snickered. "It sounds like you deserved it. Butterball is a cute, little menace."

Grey gasped. "You did not just insult my sweet piggy."

"Okay, okay, boys," Abel said. "Settle down. We need to figure out our game plan here. I think we should take out the strongest first, then go after the weakest. Grey and Justin will pounce on Carter. He won't expect it, and he won't want to hurt you guys."

"Wait, are we beating them up? That doesn't seem nice," Grey said.

"I invited Tanner. Tell me if I need to uninvite him now," Justin said, pulling out his phone. "We don't need the police there if it's going to get violent."

"Whoa," Bennett said, standing up. Yeo pressed his face into his mound of pillows, shaking with laughter. "There will be no violence. Geez, guys. What kind of club do you all have?"

"The hot mess kind," Grey said. "Obviously."

"I think, maybe you all can just distract the others while I talk with Carter," Caden said, trying to cover Linc's ears. He didn't need to hear his weird uncles plot a beat down. "I can't believe you all are ready to take them out."

"You rescued Chewie for me," Grey said. He hugged Caden from behind, pressing his face into his back.

"You came up with our pub idea," Justin said,

hugging him too. "I have a real career now, and I don't have to rely on anyone ever again."

"You accepted me for who I am," Abel said. He hugged him from the side. "I don't have to pretend when I'm around you guys."

"Look at this little foot," Grey said, grabbing Linc's foot and tugging it. The little boy giggled. "I want this foot."

The three omegas stole Linc and sat on the floor to play with Caden's son. He shook his head. He loved his friends. He really did.

A POLITE KNOCK at the door signaled the start of the weird-ass intervention. Summer, Yeo, and Tanner sat on the couch, munching on popcorn, while Bennett and Sassy played with Linc in his room. Magnolia sat on Yeo's lap, purring loudly. The cat looked at him, eyes full of judgement. Yeah, yeah. He should have tried more with Carter.

He pulled the door open, unsurprised to see a grumpy Carter surrounded by his friends. Elijah and Olive pushed Carter through the door.

"It's really strange to see you wearing a rabbit in a baby sling," Carter said, looking pointedly at Huckleberry.

"How dare you mock Huckleberry," Grey said. "Do we attack now?"

He looked back at Justin and Abel.

"No attacking," Justin said. He slid a glance to the couch. "The cops are here."

Tanner grinned and grabbed a handful of popcorn.

"Attacking? I didn't know it was that kind of intervention," Elijah said. He looked at Zoe. "We should have worn the black outfits. We would have looked tougher."

"Okay," Zoe said, pushing everyone through the door. "Clearly, we need someone to direct this thing." She pointed at Carter and Caden. "You two go to the kitchen table and sit down. Olive, go on into Linc's room and keep Uncle Bennett company." She looked at the others. "You all can mingle amongst yourselves. No attacking."

"It was Abel's idea," Grey mumbled, crossing his arms. "Harper told me I had to behave."

Zoe followed Caden and Carter to the table and sat with them.

"I can't believe you moved and didn't tell anyone," Carter said. "What the hell, Caden?"

"I didn't think about it," Caden said. "It happened quickly, and Yeo was sick. We didn't even tell the kids until today."

"I can understand that," Carter said. "You never tell me anything going on with you though. I thought that when you moved here, you'd want to be a part of my life."

"When would that be? When you were working with Juan? When you had poker nights with the guys and didn't invite me?"

"Carter!" Zoe's voice was full of censure.

"I didn't think he liked poker," Carter said. "It's not like he invited me to his weekly pub visits with his friends."

He waved his hand towards Caden's friends. Grey stood staring Ernie down. He really hoped Grey wasn't still jealous of Ernie's knitting skills. That could get messy. Justin sat in Tanner's lap, eating his popcorn, and Abel sat around the coffee table with Summer, Juan, and Ray, playing cards.

"You aren't a hot mess," Caden said. "That's the requirement to be in the club. We didn't let Zoe in either."

"You did not," she said solemnly. "It sounds like you two are jealous of the other's friends. Why do you think that is?"

Carter groaned. "I don't know. It's not like Caden ever wanted to be close to me. All we talked about in Georgia was lawyer stuff."

"That's all I talked about with anyone," Caden said. "You didn't exactly make an effort either. When you got bored, you just left. You didn't want to be there, and I knew it. Why would I try to make you stay and talk to me?"

"I... I didn't think you wanted to talk to me," Carter said. "Everyone just wanted me to make different choices. It all started to run together. You all said the same thing all the time. Law was a good and respectable profession. College was absolutely essential to a good future. The army was a waste of time."

"I never said that," Caden snapped. "That was

Mother and Father. I was proud you went your own way."

"Carter," Zoe said. "You made snap judgements about Caden and his intentions, right?"

"Yeah. I guess," Carter said, frowning.

"Caden," she said. "You're a tight-lipped butthead, right?"

He gave her a flat look. "Perhaps."

"When you two reunited, Carter had a good life with an omega and his friends here in Hobson Hills," Zoe said. "How did this make you feel, Caden?"

"Seriously?" He didn't hide his disdain.

"Answer the question," she growled.

"I don't know," he said. "Maybe I felt like there wasn't a place for me in your life."

"Good," Zoe said. "Carter, how did you feel when Caden had his epiphany at Christmas? When he decided to move here to pursue writing full-time."

"I thought it was great. I thought we'd finally have a relationship," Carter said. "Then he just started hanging out with those omegas. I saw you more when you lived in Georgia."

"Okay," Zoe said. "You both want a relationship with one another, but you're too hardheaded to take the first step. From this night forward, you will spend one night a week together, just the two of you. It can just be a few hours in your barn, Carter, but you two will bond."

"For how long," Caden asked. "Two weeks, four weeks?"

"Until I say otherwise," Zoe said. "Furthermore, you

two will be nice to each other's friends. Caden, you'll let Juan help you when you need it, and Ray is our investigator, not that other guy."

"Fuck Walter Douglas," Ray yelled from the living room.

Zoe ignored him. "Carter, you won't be snide or petty toward Grey, Abel, or Justin. They're sweet men and shouldn't be glared at. Unless it's by me."

"I really liked those shoes," Carter said, sighing.

"Butterball is just a baby, Carter," Grey said. He and Ernie were now sharing one of the large chairs, legs tangled together. They were both knitting what looked to be scarves.

"One night a week, guys. That's an order," Zoe said.

Caden looked at Carter. His brother's scarred face was flushed, and his eyes had a hint of longing in them. Maybe he needed to make an effort. He thought moving here would instantly bring them closer, but it took more than that to make a relationship work.

"Alright," Caden said.

"We'll do it," Carter said. He looked around. "Are you all going to renovate that extra space Zoe told me about? If it's like she described, you could easily add another two bedrooms and a bathroom."

"We're thinking about it," Caden said.

"Are we?" Yeo peeked over the couch. He sat with Elijah. "I thought we'd wait until more kids came along."

Zoe whined. "Caden."

"You know nothing," he told her, face stern. He

looked back at Yeo. "Can Carter come and look at it just in case?"

"Of course, baby," Yeo said, shrugging. "You can do whatever you want to it." He laughed. "Right now, Caden's keeping his…"

"Angel!" Caden yelled, interrupting his omega. "Don't tell them."

"Tell us what?" Juan turned mischievous eyes on him. "What are you hiding, Caden?"

"Nothing."

"Yeo. You have to show us," Justin said. "Please."

"I'm sorry, baby," Yeo said. "I have to do it."

"Fine," he said stoically. "Do it."

Giggling, Yeo jumped up and ran to the utility room. Everyone followed him. He opened the door leading to the unfinished space. He held the door open and everyone filed in, staring at Caden's stash.

"Caden," Carter said. "Why do you have a large amount of canned goods and toothpaste hidden away?"

"Oh look," Abel said. "You've started stocking up on toilet paper too."

# CHAPTER 10

"This leg goes in this hole, right?" Caden asked Linc.

Yeo watched Caden dress Linc and struggled not to laugh.

"Daddy, play with bun bun," Linc answered.

"We'll play with Huckleberry as soon as I figure out these pants," Caden said.

"That's a shirt," Yeo said, giving up and laughing.

"Well, that explains a few things," Caden said, chuckling. "Okay, buddy. Let's try this again."

"Are you going to write today?" Yeo watched his alpha, eyes warming as they ran over his body. He wasn't dying of a man-cold anymore, so he could fully appreciate how lucky he was. In fact, he had appreciated it twice last night and once this morning.

"Eww," Summer said, coming to stand next to him. "Stop eyeing Dad like a piece of meat."

She had taken to calling Caden dad. It had shocked the hell out of everyone. Yeo would always be her big brother, but she told them that she wanted a new dad, and Caden was her choice.

"He's my alpha to admire as I so choose," Yeo said, nose in the air.

Caden cleared his throat. "I'll be writing today, but I'm going to take Summer to school first, then run by Grey's house. I thought I'd bring Linc with so he can see the other bunnies."

"Sounds like a plan," Yeo said. "I'll be at the bookstore, but if you need me to watch Linc, just let me know."

Caden grinned at him. "We're good. I'm still his favorite."

"I can't blame him," Yeo said. "You're my favorite too."

"Again, may I say, *eww*?" Summer said. "You two are so mushy."

She hid a half-smile. The little snot knew they were adorable together.

"Are you ready for rehearsal tonight?" Yeo said, bouncing in place in excitement. His little sister was auditioning for a school play. Their parents had thought theatre was plebian and a waste of time. Their words, not his.

"Yes. You can't come, okay? I don't want you to embarrass me," Summer said.

"We won't embarrass you. We'll just peek in and watch from the back," Caden said. "No banners, Yeo."

Yeo wilted. He had the best banner ever.

"Save it for opening night, angel."

Yeo grinned. That was his honey bear.

"Horrible," Summer mumbled, leaving the room. "You two are horrible."

Yeo kissed Summer and Linc goodbye, then *kissed* his alpha goodbye. "I love you, Caden. I'll make us lunch today, okay?"

"Perfect," Caden said, and Yeo kissed him again.

"Guys, come on," Summer said, laughing. "Caden isn't going off to war."

"Fine," Yeo said and stomped to the bookstore.

Amy laughed at his pouty face. "You are ridiculous. Hey, before you go to your office, I had an idea."

"Tell me," Yeo said, lifting himself to sit on the register counter.

"Every time the town has a festival, local businesses are encouraged to participate. I was thinking we could have a booth at the spring festival in April."

"I like it," he said. "What could we sell?"

"We could do like a matchmaking game and match people to a new author or genre," Amy said. "We could also have sign-up sheets for our book clubs."

"That's a wonderful idea," he said with a smile. "Summer has been talking about starting a comic book club. She can't draw for shit, but she loves writing the stories."

"Does she not like the young adult book club?" Amy shook her head. "Damn. We have a lot of book clubs."

"We do have a lot," Yeo agreed. "Summer loves comic books more than anything in the world, though she does like the young adult group." Yeo grinned. "It's my favorite one. We're reading *Dumplin'* right now."

"Aren't you a little old for that group?"

Yeo gasped, hand to his chest. "Are you calling me old? I'm young and an adult." He hopped down. "I'm going to work on the books."

He glared at her over his shoulder, ignoring her laughter.

A few hours later and the paperwork that went with owning a business was caught up. Yeo watched the register for Amy for an hour, then grabbed the mail and headed upstairs. Caden and Linc were already back from Grey's.

"Where did that giant stuffed bunny come from?" Yeo laughed as Linc dragged the purple bunny around by its arm. It was bigger than he was. Huckleberry and Sassy followed his son around, sniffing the stuffed toy.

"Harper saw it online and had to get it for Linc," Caden said, rolling his shoulders. His alpha sat on the couch, laptop in his lap. Magnolia kept him company, the large cat stretched out along the top of the sofa. "I've just been writing an hour, but it's going well."

Yeo bent over the couch and kissed him. "That's good to hear. I'll make us lunch, then you can get back to work."

He tossed the mail on the table, then started digging in the fridge. Caden set his laptop down on the table.

"Yeo?" Caden picked up two envelopes. "This doesn't look good."

"What?" He stood straight, looking back over his shoulder.

Caden opened the first one and started reading.

"Not good." He opened the second, and his frown grew worse.

"What's wrong? What is it?"

"It looks like your ex didn't back down. She didn't retract the custody suit."

"Surely to god, she isn't that big an idiot," Yeo said in disbelief.

"She may be feeling confident, because your grandfather is suing for custody of Summer," Caden said, voice grim.

Yeo sank into a chair at the table. "They're really going to do this?"

"The court dates are close together," Caden said. "We wouldn't have to be gone long." He held Yeo's hand. "Angel, I'll take care of this. They won't get our kids."

Yeo sniffed, then looked around. Caden's words warmed him. For once in his life, he had someone in his corner. Linc sat on the floor, his rabbit propped up in front of him. He talked to it quietly, his baby words sounding like gibberish.

"I won't let them do this. We gave her a chance to back out, and she didn't." He looked up at Caden. "Will you read something for me? I have an idea."

His grandfather loved that damn company, but he didn't have control of it anymore.

"Of course," Caden said.

Yeo went to their room and dug around until he found his contract for his position at Cook Enterprises and the severance agreement he had signed. He handed both to Caden. "I didn't sign any non-solicit or noncompete agreements when they hired or fired me. I think that's why grandpa is so worried about me setting up in a similar business."

Caden read through them slowly, making notes. Yeo made lunch, and the three of them ate their egg salad sandwiches and grapes. Caden read while he ate, finally finishing to find that Linc had eaten all his grapes.

Caden gasped, looking outraged. "Thief!"

Linc just giggled and climbed off Yeo's lap to go back to his rabbit.

"It looks like you didn't sign anything even resembling a non-solicit or noncompete agreement. I'm surprised your father approved these documents."

"He never reads anything," Yeo said. "I drew them up, and he signed them. It would never occur to him that I would do anything to hurt the company."

"What do you want to do?" Caden pulled him into his arms, holding him close. Yeo leaned his head against Caden's chest and listened to his steady heartbeat.

"I don't want to go to court if we can help it. I don't want to upset the kids," Yeo said. "My dad can stop this. He just needs a little motivation to get involved."

"I take it you have a way to motivate him?" Caden stroked his back.

"Let's make a call," Yeo said. They sat at the couch, and Yeo called his dad, setting his iPhone to record and putting it on speaker.

"Yeo? What do you want?" His father sounded tired and old. The new guy must really not be working out.

"Grandpa is suing for custody of Summer, and my

lovely ex-wife is suing for custody of Linc," Yeo said. "We have a problem."

"It's not my problem," Michael said, grumbling. "Dad mentioned something about camps to fix Summer. I don't care."

"You had best start caring," Yeo said. "You didn't read my severance agreement, did you?"

"What are you talking about?"

"Let's see," Yeo said, tapping his chin. "Paul Cross and his company like to feel involved in the ordering process. I think I should call him and let him know that the salespeople at Jacobs Manufacturing have wonderful people skills. He'd be much better suited ordering from them."

"What the fuck are you talking about? Cross just called to complain yesterday," Michael said. "How did you know that?"

"I know the idiot you hired," Yeo said. "He may be better than Derek, but not by much. Cross isn't one to sit back and accept a less than stellar experience."

"You can't call him. We'd lose his account."

"Like I give a damn. If you don't want me to call each and every one of your large accounts and recommend they go to one of your rivals, you'll do what I say."

"What do you want?" Michael sounded tired again.

"You will make grandpa cancel the custody suit. Make it clear that I will ruin the fucking company if you don't," Yeo said. "My alpha is a magnificent lawyer and would love to tear the bastard a new one, but I'd rather this be taken care of quietly."

"Fine. I'll talk to him," his father said. "You have an alpha?" His voice dripped with disgust. "I take it you won't be coming back?"

"I'd rather become a panhandler in Antarctica. Let me know when he withdraws his petition."

"I'll deal with Dad, but there's nothing I can do about Tracy."

"Oh, I don't need your help for her," Yeo said sweetly. "There is one other thing."

"What?"

"Lowell. I want two weeks with him in the summer. I'll pay for his flights. He's our brother, and we miss him."

"I don't want him corrupted," Michael said.

"He's sixteen and has a brain of his own. Do you want your company to fail?"

"Fine. Two weeks and two weeks only," he said, obviously gritting his teeth.

The call ended, and Caden hugged him. "How did that feel, angel?"

"So good," Yeo said. "I never stood up to him until Summer did. Do you know she had to live in a group home until we met with the judge? It was horrible. I lost any desire to please that bastard when he did that."

"I don't blame you," Caden said, rubbing his shoulders. "What do you want to do about Tracy? She has zero chance of winning."

"I shouldn't find this fun," Yeo said. He called Fawn, putting her on speakerphone. "Hey, pretty lady."

"Yeo," she said. "It's so nice to hear from you. How is Summer doing?"

"Good. She's auditioning for the role of Juliet tonight at school. She's really good."

"Oh." Fawn sounded surprised. "I didn't know she was interested in theatre."

"I'll record her audition and send it to you," he said.

"Thank you, Yeo," Fawn said, voice soft. "Now, why did you call? Your grandpa and that nasty woman you married have been spending a lot of time together. Poor Derek doesn't know what the hell he's gotten into."

"Tracy wants to sue for custody of Linc."

"What! She isn't even his mother," Fawn said.

"You know that? I thought I kept it hidden," Yeo said, surprised.

"Sweetie, you despise that woman. Why would you go on a four month cruise with her? Plus, you came back with a baby," Fawn said.

"Everyone thought she didn't want anyone to see her big and pregnant," Yeo said.

"While that is easy to believe, I know that woman. There is no way she would have the patience to grow a baby knowing it would mess up her perfect figure." Her voice grew fond. "I know you too, sweetie. You've wanted children ever since I got you that baby doll when you were three. You pushed it around in your toy stroller and asked for more babies."

Caden laughed. "I bet you were adorable."

Fawn gasped. "Who is that?"

She sounded tickled.

"This is Caden," Yeo said proudly. "He's my alpha.

Summer calls him dad, Fawn. You're still mom, but she wants to forget Dad."

"Oh, I don't blame her," Fawn said. "It's nice to meet you, Caden. I'm so glad you and Yeo are there for Summer. I love my girl."

Yeo tried to push back the thought that if she loved her, she would never have stayed with that bastard. Fawn made a choice when she married Michael Cook, and she stood by it, no matter what.

"We have a favor to ask," Yeo said. "I need you to let free a little information."

"That sounds like fun," Fawn said. "Do you want me to call all her friends and tell them what a rotten liar she is?"

Yeo slumped. She'd taken all his dramatic fun away. "That was my plan," he said. "I have pictures of her in… uh… compromising positions, but I feel sleazy using those against her. I mean, I will if I have to, but I'd rather try the truth about Linc's birth first."

"Is one of those pictures of her and your dad? I know they were together," Fawn said.

"Yeah," Yeo said, reluctantly. His dad's affairs were an embarrassment to Fawn, and he didn't want to make her feel bad.

"I'm tempted to *borrow* those pictures from you," she said, then sighed. "I will be happy to spread the news of Linc's birth. Give me a day, then call her. Tell the bitch that if she doesn't retract that suit, I'll send those pictures to her friends."

"Thank you, Fawn," he said. "I also bargained with

Dad to get Lowell two weeks with us over the summer. You are more than welcome to join us."

"I'll think about it, baby boy," she said. Yeo had a feeling she'd stay right where she was. He wished for the millionth time that Fawn Cook was a stronger woman.

# CHAPTER 11

Caden watched his omega move above him. Yeo rode Caden, his ass tight around Caden's dick. His liquid black eyes were soft and adoring as he stared down at him. Their bodies moved together perfectly, Caden's fingers on Yeo's hips and Yeo's hands braced on his chest.

Their eyes stayed locked when Yeo came with a whimper, splattering against Caden's stomach. He pushed into his omega three more times, then filled him as he came. Yeo leaned down, pressing his forehead to Caden's.

"Having you in me is like being a full moon," Yeo said.

"Huh?" Caden's brain wasn't quite functioning.

"Don't worry about it," Yeo said, kissing him softly. "I love you so damn much, Caden. How did this happen? How did we get so lucky?"

"It wasn't my romancing skills," Caden said.

"You romanced me perfectly," Yeo said. "It was

honest, awkward, and real. I never thought I'd trust an alpha after seeing how the shitty ones in my family acted." He rolled to his side, propping his head on Caden's shoulder. Caden's heart felt full with his omega in his arms. "I don't get why everyone says you're distant and uncaring."

Caden kissed Yeo's wet forehead. "Who says that?"

"Some of the customers that come in. The whole town knows we're together, and they all have an opinion. Even Zoe and Bennett seem surprised every time you smile," Yeo said.

"How do you see me?"

"Sweet, passionate, so full of love," Yeo said, humming. "You're my family, Caden. You, Linc, and Summer. You all are my family, and I can't get over how much I love you." He looked up, meeting Caden's eyes. "When I worked for Dad, I had to wear a mask. I couldn't feel anything, and I think, after a while, I died inside. Having Linc restarted my heart. Being here with you all makes me feel like I can do anything."

"Yeo," Caden said, voice hoarse. "I swear you're my soul speaking. People don't see how we're alike, but we are. You weren't the only one who wore a mask. I just happen to still wear mine most of the time."

"I don't like it," Yeo said, kissing his chin. "No more masks, Caden. It may be comfortable, but that's only because it's what you're familiar with."

"I'll do my best, angel, but I may need you to remind me." He stroked Yeo's face, thumb running over that sassy pointed chin. "I'm so proud of you. You took care of everything. I just got to flex my lawyer muscles by being present."

"I won't let anyone take you all away from me," Yeo said.

"I wish I could have fought for you though. I'm proud of you, but I would have enjoyed proving my love."

Yeo laughed. "You nursed me through a man-cold. You already proved your love, baby."

"Are you guys going to get up? It's already seven," Summer said, banging on the door. "Linc is sitting in the litter box again. Huckleberry is with him."

"Shit," Yeo said, jumping out of bed and throwing some sweats and a t-shirt on. "Why is he so obsessed with the litter box?"

"Hopefully, it's still empty," Caden said, laughing. He got up and pulled some clothes on. "I cleaned it last night. Of course, Huck may be about to poop on Linc."

"Eww, I think Linc used the litter box," Summer said. "Juliet did not have to deal with this crap. Literally."

"No," Yeo wailed, running out the door. "That's not how we want you to use the potty, Linc!"

Summer's eyes met Caden's, and they started laughing.

"Oh god, this is too funny," Summer said. "At least he didn't poop in the yard like Sassy."

"Wait until summertime. He may surprise us. I think it's time we put the litter box up out of his reach," Caden side, wiping his eyes and wheezing.

"Huckleberry has a box in his rabbit condo, so he can use that. Magnolia *can* jump."

He watched Yeo walk past with Linc. His nose was squished up, and he held the little naked boy straight out from him. Caden started laughing again.

"You suck, Caden," Yeo yelled from Linc's bathroom.

"I love you, angel," he called back, chuckling. "What do you want for breakfast, Summer?"

"Waffles. Will you drive me to school?"

"Of course." Caden loved mornings. It had been two weeks since Richard and Tracy had withdrawn their suits, and his family had a routine. He took care of the mornings and getting everyone moving. Yeo, Linc, and he ate lunch together, and then Yeo handled dinner while he helped Summer study her lines for the play. He would have made a damn good Romeo.

Caden took a freshly bathed Linc with him when he took Summer to school. Yeo looked like he needed a break. He took his time driving home after getting Summer to school. The town was still in the grips of winter, but with the holidays over, everyone was just trying to stay warm and survive until spring. It was supposedly the most miserable time of the year, but Caden had never been happier. He grinned as he parked and got Linc out of the car.

They made their way into the bookstore, and he looked around for Yeo. Amy waved at him from the register. She looked worried. "Caden. Some man showed up and yelled at Yeo. There were customers around, so Yeo took him back to the office. I don't like the way he looked at Yeo. I called Tanner."

"Thanks, Amy," Caden said, worry punching into his gut. "Watch Linc, please?"

"Of course," she said, holding her arms out for the little boy. "Your daddy will make the mean man go away."

He could hear the man's loud voice from the register. He ran to the office and threw open the door. He watched in horror as the man pulled his fist back to hit Yeo. He was too far away. He rushed forward, but the man never touched Caden's omega. Yeo dodged the punch and grabbed the man's arm, twisting.

"Derek, what the hell?" Yeo sounded furious. "You don't get to lay a fucking hand on me. I kicked your ass when we were kids, and I'll do it again if you don't back the fuck off."

"Fuck you," Derek said. The man was red-faced. His light brown hair and hazel eyes matched Summer's, but he had a big, soft frame and a mulish expression. "You ruin everything. You always have."

"You tried to help Tracy take my son from me," Yeo said. "Do you honestly expect me to feel guilty?"

"She left me, because you turned everyone against her," Derek yelled. "That's what you do. You turned Dad and Grandpa against me. You even turned Mom against me. She yelled at me for helping Tracy. Yelled! I was helping a lady get custody of her child, but she yelled at me."

Yeo looked tired. "Derek, you have to know Tracy

never wanted Linc. You aren't that stupid. Fawn told you the truth, right?"

"She still loved him," Derek said. "You had no right!"

"Loved him? She didn't want anything to do with him, you idiot."

"That's not true. She said he was her link to you, and she loved you more than anything," Derek said. Caden winced. That had to have pissed Derek off to no end.

"Derek, she never loved me. She loved being married to one of Richard Cook's grandsons. She fucked around constantly. I have pictures of her with several different men, including Dad and Grandpa. She is a user and a manipulator."

Derek shook his head. "That's not true. You're lying. She isn't like that."

"Why did you never tell me you loved her?" Yeo reached out to the man, but Derek pushed away. "Ours was just a marriage of convenience. I had more with my Caden after a few days then I did with her after five years of marriage."

"I hate you so fucking much. Everything goes perfectly for you," Derek said. Caden's heart froze. This could have been Carter and him. Damn.

"Nothing went the way I wanted it to until I left Tennessee with Summer and Linc," Yeo said. "I tried for years to be what Dad and Grandpa wanted. I wanted Dad to not regret taking me in when I was born." Yeo shook his head. "It was useless, Derek. Nothing will make them happy. Nothing. To them, I was always the omega they had to hide away. I did my best to become useful to them. I ran their company, but that wasn't enough either. They aren't worthy of us. They don't deserve our love or our loyalty. Neither does Tracy."

Caden pulled up the pictures of Tracy and Richard on his phone and handed it to Derek. The man looked at it, eyes watering. He sobbed and shoved his fist in his mouth, biting down hard. Caden and Yeo both moved, wrapping the man in their arms. Derek broke, burying his face against Yeo. They stood with him for a long time, letting him cry. Caden knew how the man felt. He knew what it was like to be a hot mess.

Slowly, they drifted apart. Yeo kept Derek's hand in his.

"I hate them," Derek finally said. "All I wanted was for them to like me. They didn't even have to love me."

"I felt the same for a long time," Yeo said.

"I hate the company. I hate the idea of being trapped inside all day," Derek said, shaking. "Fuck. What am I going to do? Tracy had plans for us. I... I'm not good at making plans."

"What makes you happy, Derek," Caden asked. "What's something that makes you smile?"

The man thought for a while. Yeo just patiently held his hand. "I like to do projects around the house, especially in the yard. Dad gets mad when I do though. He says wealthy men don't mow the grass, and alphas don't sniff flowers."

"Fuck him," Caden said. "Think about what makes *you* happy and spend some time doing it. See where it takes you."

Derek gave a half-hearted smile. "You sound like you're talking from experience."

Yeo laughed. "You would be right."

"I don't want to go home," Derek said, closing his eyes. "I made up my mind that everything that was wrong was your fault, Yeo."

"Stay here for a while," Yeo said. "It's a nice town."

"No," Derek said, shaking his head. "I can't do that." He looked at Yeo, guilt filling his eyes. "I did something really bad."

"You thought Linc was her beloved son," Yeo said. "I get it."

"Not that," Derek said, shaking his head. "I was at Mom and Dad's one night. The phone rang, and I answered it before Mom could. It was your papa. He asked for you, and I told him you had decided you didn't want to talk to him anymore. I told him to never call there again. When Mom asked who it was, I said Grandpa. She doesn't know."

Yeo whimpered, dropping Derek's hand, devastation filling his eyes. "Why would you do that? Papa uses a burner phone every time. There's no way I can call him back. Why would you do that?"

"I'm so sorry," Derek said. He closed his eyes and tears rolled down his face. "Your papa wanted you. He loved you enough to go against his alpha and call you all the time. I was so jealous, Yeo. I'm so sorry."

Yeo sat in his desk chair and cried. Caden moved him around, sat, and held him in his lap. "It'll be alright, angel. Ray is looking for your papa, remember?"

"I'm going to go," Derek said, looking miserable. "I'll see if I can find him, Yeo. I'll try to fix this."

"I'll text you Ray's number," Caden said. "If you find anything at your father's house that might tell us how to reach Yeo's papa, call him."

"I will. I'm so sorry." Derek turned and ran from the room.

"Papa thinks I hate him, Caden," Yeo said. "I know that has to hurt him so much."

"We'll find him," Caden said. "We'll make this right."

# CHAPTER 12

Yeo deducted fifteen hundred dollars plus shipping from the store's account. He tried to feel excited about purchasing the comic book collection from the young man in Ohio. He couldn't manage it. He knew there would be treasures to sort through, as well as junk, which usually made him happy.

All he could think about for the past week was Papa thinking he hated him. He scratched his stomach again. Ray had said that he'd found a copy of Papa's marriage certificate, his four children's birth certificates, and his alpha's death certificate. There was a police report about the alpha's death. Three months ago, someone shot him while he was out at a bar. Otherwise, he wasn't finding much. He had some contacts at the police that were on vacation. Ray hoped they might be able to give him more. Derek hadn't been able to find anything at Dad's house. Fawn had looked too. His stepmom was almost as upset as Yeo. She knew how much his papa loved him.

"Yeo," Amy said. "Were you able to order more Nolen Judd mysteries? Mr. Thomas bought copies of each of them, and he'll like them and suggest them to his buddies." She stood in the door of his office. "Are you alright, sweetie?"

"My stupid stomach keeps itching," he said, sniffling. He didn't care about his dry skin. He wanted to talk to his papa. Their conversations were never long or in-depth, but they were special.

"Can I take a look?" Amy walked closer.

Yeo didn't say anything. He pulled his shirt up, showing her his dry skin. He really needed to exercise more. His stomach was pooching out a bit.

"Yeo! Look at your omega line."

He frowned and looked down. It was a little swollen and bright pink. The skin around it was dry and flaky. Wait.

"I'm pregnant," he whispered, hope filling him. "Shit. I'm pregnant."

"How long has your stomach been itching?"

"A while," he answered. "I need to make a doctor's appointment to make sure. What if I just have some strange disease?"

"Call Dr. Richards right now," Amy said. She looked out at the store. "I need to go ring someone up." She gave him a no-nonsense look. "If he has an opening today, take it."

"Yes, ma'am." Yeo smiled for the first time that

week. He grabbed his phone. Shit. "Amy! What's his number?"

An hour and a half later, he sat in the waiting room, playing games on his phone. He hadn't said anything to Caden. His alpha was writing and keeping an eye on Linc. Yeo didn't want to get his hopes up if he just had a fatal disease.

"Mr. Cook?"

Yeo looked up. A nurse waited on him. He stood and followed her back. She asked him a few questions and took some tests, then left him in the room. After a while, Dr. Richards came in, smiling. "Mr. Cook, congratulations."

"I'm pregnant?"

"Yes. I'd like to do a few tests, if you don't mind."

"Sure," Yeo said, grinning. He was pregnant. Caden and he would have another baby. Oh, he wished Caden was here.

"Yeo!" Caden pushed in the door. "Am I too late?"

"Can you read minds?" Yeo asked, eyeing his alpha suspiciously.

"With Zoe and Amy nearby, I don't need to read minds," Caden said, standing next to him, holding his hand.

They heard the baby's heartbeat and had the first ultrasound done. He was almost two months pregnant, and the baby looked like a tiny peanut.

"That's our peanut," Yeo said, kissing Caden's cheek.

"You look fine," Dr. Richards said. "You lucked out with no morning sickness. Make sure you take your vitamins and eat well. Get plenty of rest. You're going to be tired a lot for the next while. I'd like to see you again in two months."

They left the doctor's office, and Caden picked him up and spun him around in the parking lot. "We're having a baby. Do you think it'll be a boy or girl? What are we going to name it? Oh god. We need to get a nursery set up. Do you think Linc will mind having a younger sibling? He used the potty today."

"Whoa," Yeo said, laughing. "We have time to figure things out. Now, tell me about Linc using the potty. It wasn't in the litter box again?"

"No. It was in his potty chair," Caden said, smiling. "He's a little angel. Just like you."

"*I* don't use the litter box."

"He was just copying his role model – Magnolia."

"Don't make excuses for the little stinker. Speaking of, where is he?"

"Aunt Zoe is on duty. She's probably stuffing him full of cookies as we speak," Caden said.

They looked at one another in horror.

"We need to get back."

THAT NIGHT, Yeo cooked biscuits and gravy. He was having a baby, and he wanted biscuits and gravy.

"You make the best biscuits," Summer said. "Mom and Asshole's cook never made them this well."

"They're angel biscuits," Yeo said, squeezing Caden's hand. "There's a restaurant outside of Nashville that makes them."

"Angel biscuits. Of course, they're angel biscuits if you made them," Caden said. "Hopefully, you'll crave these all the time while you're pregnant."

"Knowing our luck, he'll probably crave pickles and salmon patties or something like that," Summer said.

Yeo stuck his tongue out at his sister. "How is school going?"

"You see my grades," she said, teasingly. "Really, it's going well. I didn't know if I'd like a new school in a new town, but, so far, everyone is either nice or indifferent."

"I suppose having Hannah around helps," Caden said, hiding his smile when Summer blushed.

"Hannah is… Hannah is something else," Summer said. "I've never met someone so passionate about life. She's genuine, you know? She's so kind. If I hurt, she hurts. If I'm happy, she's happy."

"You really like her," Yeo said. He wondered if it was more than a kid's crush.

"I don't think there's anyone like her in all the world," Summer said. "I didn't feel like this when I was crushing on Misty Butler back in Tennessee. This is more, guys. I think I'll either marry her or be her best friend for the rest of my life. Either way, Hannah and I are a team."

"That's great," Yeo said. "Be careful though. Make sure you two are on the same page. I'd hate for you to get your heart broken."

Sassy started barking when someone knocked on the door. Linc was sitting on Caden's lap, so Yeo went to see who it was. *It best not be another well-intentioned intervention*, Yeo thought. Carter had talked Caden into completely renovating the remaining space, which would take time and be noisy. Ray stood at the door and smiled widely when Yeo answered the door.

"Hi, Ray."

"I found your papa," Ray said.

Yeo squealed and jumped the poor man, scaring the crap out of him. He wrapped his arms around Ray's neck and hugged him hard. "Do you have his number? Can I call him?"

"We need to talk first," Ray said. "There's some stuff you need to know."

"Come in." Yeo pulled the large beta into the kitchen. "Sit down. Do you want some biscuits and gravy?"

"Oh, fuck yes," Ray said, taking a sniff of the plate of warm biscuits. "Are these homemade?"

"Sure are," Summer said. She dished him up a plate and set it in front of him. "You want some orange juice?"

"Thanks," he said. "That would be great."

He started shoveling food in his mouth but took breaks to fill Yeo in. "My buddy from the Jackson Police Department finally got back to me. He knew right away what was going on. Your papa's alpha was a real doomsday, conspiracy theorist nut job. He kept the family completely off the grid right outside Jackson. They had a tiny farm there."

"That explains why he couldn't call me more," Yeo said.

"His alpha wasn't fond of you, that's for sure. I

talked to a few of their neighbors and more than one told me he would often rant about loose omegas and the devil spawn they made."

"Aww, you're a cute devil spawn," Summer said, patting his shoulder.

"He wasn't good to your papa or your siblings either," Ray said. "He beat on your papa and wouldn't let him go to the hospital. Your poor papa has scars all over his face. One of the neighbors said the alpha liked to use a broken beer bottle on him."

"No," Yeo said, covering his mouth. His papa needed him. He would never let anyone hurt him again.

"The last year was the worst. Your papa had four children with him, but they were all omega boys. From what I understand, the fucker got tired of him and started screwing any woman or omega he could, hoping to get an alpha son," Ray said.

"That bastard," Caden said. "How did he treat the boys?"

"From what I can tell, Yeo's papa protected them from any physical abuse."

"The alpha is dead now, right?" Yeo had never been happier about someone's death. There were more ways to hurt children than with your fists. He imagined they'd suffered plenty.

"Yeah. My buddy said they were still investigating, but it looked like it was a jealous spouse. The alpha was handsome, even if he was an asshole. He managed to get around."

"How is Papa?" Yeo wanted to go get him and hold him forever.

"Not so great," Ray said. "When his alpha died, they lost the farm. The fucker owed a lot of money to some shady-ass people. The man didn't believe in educating omegas either, and he kept them all under his thumb. Your papa has no education and was seldom allowed to even leave the house. I don't know if he's able to do a lot of physical work with his injuries."

"Are they alright right now? How are they living?" Summer had tears in her eyes. Hannah wasn't the only sweet and kind teenager around.

"Yeo's oldest half-brother is twenty, and he is working hard as a dishwasher in Jackson to support them all. The other three are sixteen, twelve, and nine. They're all staying in a house right next to their old farm," Ray said. "It's really sad. They were apparently attached to the critters they kept on the farm, but they can't afford to take care of them. One of the neighbors took the animals, so they at least get to visit them."

"Caden," Yeo said, looking to his alpha.

"I have a large lake cabin with several acres standing empty, and you need to hire some more people for the store," Caden said. "Can you take off a few days so we can go get them?"

"I love you, Caden Benson," Yeo said. He had one amazing alpha.

"I want to go," Summer said. "We'll need to get a ton of trailers, and we'll need to buy back their pets from that neighbor. Is the land fenced in at the lake cabin, Dad?"

"No, but Grey and Harper probably won't mind storing some pets until we can get a fence and barn up,"

Caden said. He would need a lot of drivers, or he would need to hire some people.

"You had best call your brother for help before you call Tanner or your buddies," Ray said. "A whole trip with your brother would count for a lot of weekly bonding times. Zoe will approve." The large beta gave Yeo a big-eyed, puppy dog look. "Can I have seconds?"

# CHAPTER 13

Caden drove Marco's truck while Carter slept in the passenger seat. They pulled a large horse trailer behind them. Huckleberry rode in a carrier between them. Caden's bunny hadn't wanted to be left behind with Zoe like Sassy and Magnolia. Carter had teased him when he saw the rabbit, but Caden didn't care. *Yeo didn't blink an eye at Huck*, Caden thought, smirking. His omega was a good one.

Bennett's alpha had lent them four of his trailers plus his truck. Marco had wanted to come, but he couldn't find someone to take care of his cattle last minute. Gramps and Grammy pulled another trailer, and Ray and Juan pulled a third. Tanner and Justin pulled the last trailer. Caden hoped there was enough space to carry any animals Yeo's papa and brothers wanted to keep. From what Ray said, there were quite a few. Dean's little farm had been full of animals.

Yeo and Bennett drove Harper's Jeep. Summer, Linc, and Hannah rode with them. Caden smiled, thinking about the last gas stop. Bennett and Yeo were so damn sweet together. Yeo had told his best friend about the baby, and the last time Caden saw them, they were giggling and planning the nursery.

Abel, Grey, and the rest of the Wilsons were getting the cabin ready. It was smaller than his parents' cabin, but it had three bedrooms and two bathrooms. The bedrooms were large, though, so maybe the boys wouldn't mind sharing. Gramps had already found a place for Yeo's oldest half-brother in case he wanted to live on his own.

Caden looked at Carter. His brother hadn't even hesitated in agreeing to come with him. They hadn't spoken much, but it was a twenty-hour drive, and they weren't stopping, so one of them needed to be sleeping when the other wasn't. It was nice, though, knowing Carter had his back.

They arrived outside Jackson at seven in the morning on Saturday. Carter dropped Caden and Huck off at Dean's house, then the trucks and trailers headed to the neighbor's house. Ray had already spoken with him about taking the animals. Dean and his boys had four horses, two milk cows, a donkey, three miniature pigs, and a bunch of chickens. They also had three dogs, four cats, and two hamsters.

It had bothered Yeo quite a bit to know his brothers had to give up their precious pets. Frankly, it surprised Caden that Dean's alpha had let them have so many pets. The man didn't sound like a loving father and husband. Caden looked around. The house was tiny and rundown. Despite that, the yard was clean and neat, even in late March.

Yeo carried Linc and jogged over to Caden, waiting as he strapped Huckleberry into his sling. "What if Papa doesn't want to see me? What if he doesn't want to move?" He bit his lip. "Should I have called first?"

"Ray couldn't find a number, angel," Caden reminded him. "Don't worry. He loves you."

"Come on, Yeo," Bennett said. "Don't you want to see your papa?"

"Yes," Yeo said, longing filling his voice.

"We're so close to Nashville," Summer said. "I wish we'd known he'd lived here before. We could have visited him. We could have been sneaky about it."

"Come on, angel." Caden took his hand, and they walked to the door.

A man opened the door before they arrived. He was older, in his late forties. His features told Caden this was Yeo's papa. He looked like an older version of Caden's omega, with white hair at his temples and a few lines at his eyes. There was uncertainty and confusion in Dean's black eyes. A hand rose to cover the ugly scars on his face.

"Papa?" Yeo pulled Caden forward, running to his omega father. The man stared in disbelief but opened his arms to catch his son.

"Yeo? What are you doing here?" He leaned back and cupped Yeo's face. Tears started to stream down the man's scarred cheeks. "You're so beautiful, baby boy. Look at you."

He hugged Yeo and Linc tight. Caden was content

to let Yeo use his hand, even if it was held at an awkward angle now.

"I don't hate you, Papa." Yeo spoke too fast, words jumbling together. "Derek lied to you on the phone. I had to change my number because I moved, but Fawn was going to give you my new number. I love you, Papa. I swear."

"Oh," Dean said, rubbing his cheek to his son's. "I didn't think you hated me, baby boy. I planned on calling back another time."

"Promise?"

"Yes." He looked Linc over. "This is Lincoln? He looks just like you!"

"Like you both," Caden said, smiling softly.

Dean smiled, pleased. "He does, doesn't he?"

"Papa?" A young man looked over Dean's shoulder. He looked exhausted and rubbed the sleep from his eyes.

"Jackson, this is your older brother, Yeo," Dean said. "This is your nephew, Lincoln."

"Damn," Jackson said. "You two look just like Papa, Jimmy, and Grandpapa." Yeo's brother was short but sturdy. He had light brown skin, green eyes, and a ton of freckles. He grinned at Yeo and reached for Linc's foot, giving it a tug. "Hey there, buddy. I should watch my mouth, huh?"

"Come in, come in," Dean said. "I can't believe I've left y'all at the door."

He tugged them inside, then waved Bennett, Summer, and Hannah in too. *This house is tiny,* Caden thought. He could probably fit three of these in his lake cabin. It was neat and clean, though, even if it was sparse.

"This is Caden," Yeo said, holding up their joined hands. "He's my alpha."

"Nice rabbit," Jackson said, smirking.

"Rabbit?" Two boys ran over from the kitchen. The youngest one reached out and stroked Huck's ears.

"He's so soft," the little boy said. He looked like a miniature of Jackson.

"His name is Huckleberry," Hannah said. "Isn't he adorable?"

"We've never had a rabbit before," the other boy said. He stroked along Huck's back. "He really is cute."

Yeo's middle brother looked different from the others. He had some of Dean's features, but he also had blue eyes and reddish brown hair. He was also covered in freckles.

"This is my sister/daughter, Summer, and her best friend, Hannah," Yeo continued, excited. He let go of Caden and ran to Bennett. "Papa, this is my best friend, Bennett. We're both pregnant!" He bounced in place as he stared at the boys playing with Huck. "Are these my brothers too?"

Dean's low laugh was rich and delighted. "This is Julian." He pointed to the youngest. "We call him Jules." He patted the older boy's shoulder. "This guy is Jacob, but we call him Jake." He pointed toward the short hallway. "James, or Jimmy if you prefer, is still sleeping. He's a grumpy teenager, so we let him sleep in on Saturdays."

Dean limped over to the couch, pulling Yeo along.

"Please, everyone, have a seat. Jackson, bring the chairs in from the kitchen. So, you're going to have another baby? That's wonderful." He looked at Caden. "You're his alpha?" His eyes caught on Huckleberry. "I guess you can't be too bad."

"He's wonderful," Yeo said, sitting with his papa. "He writes romance novels and does very well for himself. More importantly, he's kind and loves me and the kids."

"He is so unromantic, Mr. Dean," Summer said. "You should have seen him courting Yeo. He gave him milk and butter. Milk. And. Butter."

Dean just laughed. "Very practical."

Caden blushed. He unstrapped Huckleberry and set him on the floor. Hannah, Jake, and Summer sat around the rabbit, petting and pampering the spoiled thing. Jules sat next to Yeo, scooting in close and laying his head on his arm. Damn. Caden really wanted to hug that kid.

"Baby boy, I'm so happy for you," Dean said. "It's hard to remember that not every alpha is a bad egg."

"I know what you mean," Yeo said. "It took some convincing for me to give him a chance at first. Of course, I couldn't resist that bunny." He hugged Linc to him. "My son couldn't resist them either."

"We used to have a lot of pets," Jules said, holding Yeo's hand. "I had a piggy named Petunia. I love her so much. Mr. Chris and Ms. Wendy let us visit them at their farm."

Yeo looked nervous. "I heard you all had a lot of pets when you lived next door."

"We did, but we can't feed them, and there's no room here," Jules said sadly. "We had to do what was best for them."

"That was a very mature decision," Bennett said. "It's hard letting go of loved ones, even if it's the best thing for them."

Yeo looked at his papa. "There's a reason I'm here," he said and looked at Jackson. The young omega sat at one of the kitchen chairs. "Do you like your job at Texas Roadhouse?"

"I wash dishes," Jackson said dryly. "It's a job, but it's just a job."

"Well, you see," Yeo said. "I just opened a bookstore. I have one employee, but I could really use another person or two. Would you be interested?"

Jackson's eyes glowed for a second, then dimmed. "We don't have the money to move. Mr. Chris lets us stay here for dirt cheap, and, honestly, it's what we can afford."

"We had some friends drive down with us," Caden said. "We have livestock trailers for your animals and boxes for your things. I have a cabin and some acreage sitting empty about fifteen minutes from Hobson Hills." He looked Dean in the eye. "Yeo would love to have his papa nearby. Please come with us."

Dean's eyes watered. He looked at Jackson. "Can we? I know I'm useless and need your help with the boys, but can we please do this?"

"Yes, Papa," Jackson said, tears in his own eyes. He jumped up to hug his father. "I know it hurts you to not be a part of his life." He glared at Dean for a second and gently shook him. "Don't say you're useless. You take care of everyone. On the farm, you did all the work. Dad did shit. Sure, you were slow at it, but it got done."

"You boys helped too," Dean said, wiping his eyes. "We can go with Yeo?"

"We'll start packing," Jackson said. "A bookstore sounds a lot better than washing dishes." He grinned at Yeo. "Plus, I have a nephew and niece to spoil."

Jules leaned over and whispered in Linc's ear. "I'm your uncle. I'll play with you lots, okay?" He sat up with a trembling lip "Wait. Did you say we can take the animals? Petunia can be mine again? My hamsters too?"

Yeo wrapped his arm around him. "Yes. Petunia and your hamsters are all yours. Caden's brother and a lot of our friends are loading everyone up now."

Jules whooped and jumped up. "I'm waking up Jimmy. He'll be so happy. He loves Cheddar and Gouda."

He ran into one of rooms, and Caden could hear him jump on his brother. Wait. Cheddar and Gouda?

Jake laughed at Caden. "You look so confused. Cheddar and Gouda are Jimmy's horses. They're appaloosas."

"Oh. I thought he just really liked cheese," Summer said, shrugging. "Hannah and I are going to help Jake pack, okay?"

"That would be nice of you," Caden said. "I'll go get boxes out of the Jeep."

"I'll help you," Jackson said. They walked to the Jeep and opened the back. It was full of cardboard boxes from the bookstore. Jackson grabbed a few. "Are you sure you don't mind us staying at your cabin?"

Caden set his stack down and faced Jackson. "I *want* Yeo's family to live at the cabin. I love him and want his papa nearby. He didn't even think about you all wanting to get to know him. This is perfect." He awkwardly patted Jackson's shoulder. "Gramps found a place for you in town too. You're twenty. You may actually want to be on your own."

Jackson shook his head. "I have to pay the utilities and rent. I can't do that on two places."

"Jackson, you aren't paying rent on the cabin. I own it. Plus, Yeo and I want to help Dean too. You aren't alone in this."

Jackson swallowed hard, tears in his eyes. "It's been so hard here. Everyone in the neighborhood knows what Dad did to Papa. Mr. Chris and Ms. Wendy are the only ones who ever tried to help. A lot of people in town don't like omegas or think they should work. It was hard to find a job. Papa couldn't find anything. No one wanted him. I hate being named after this stupid town."

"A bunch of idiots," Caden said, snorting. He looked around. Good. No one heard him snort. "You'll like the bookstore. Will Dean be able to handle all the animals you guys have?"

"Oh yeah," Jackson said. "He loved taking care of the farm. We had a ton of cattle he cared for. That's how we paid the bills. Dad didn't do anything."

"I've been meaning to ask," Caden said, and they started carrying the boxes in. "Why did your papa give

Yeo a Korean name, but you all got non-Korean names?"

"Neither Grandpa nor Dad would let Grandpapa or Papa do anything *foreign*." Jackson laughed. "Grandpa, basically, ordered a mail-order omega from Korea, then didn't want him to be Korean."

"My Dad is an idiot," Dean said, taking the boxes from them.

"How did you come up with Yeo's name?" Bennett was taking dishes and pans out of cabinets and placing them on the counter. Yeo sat on the floor with Linc and Huckleberry.

"When I was little, my papa told me about his little brother back in South Korea. He missed him so much, but Dad wouldn't let him call or visit. His name was Yeo."

Yeo looked up, so full of happiness that Caden couldn't help but lean down and kiss him.

"Eww," Jules said. "They're making kissy faces out here, Jimmy."

He ran back into the bedroom. Yeo laughed, and Caden dipped down again and kissed him more thoroughly.

"Yeo, Dad," Summer said, jumping up and down beside them. "Jimmy draws! He's really good too, and he likes the sound of the stories I've written. We're going to make comic books together. It's going to be so awesome."

Caden had never seen her so excited.

She hopped up and down, then grabbed some boxes from Jackson. "Hurry up! We have to get them home."

"The cabin has a small attic with a bunch of windows," Caden said, musing. "I wonder if Carter could turn it into a room for Jimmy. Artists need natural light, right?"

Yeo gave him a warm look, and Dean made a small noise and covered his mouth. He limped to Caden and hugged him tightly. Caden blinked in surprise but slowly wrapped his arms around Yeo's papa.

"I'm glad Yeo found you, Caden," Dean whispered.

# CHAPTER 14

*Y*eo dug into his plate of biscuits and gravy. "I told you these were the best biscuits," he said around his mouthful of food.

They were on the way home but had stopped for breakfast at his favorite diner outside of Nashville. Dean and his boys didn't have a lot of belongings, just the basics and their pets, so it hadn't taken them long to pack.

Gramps and Grammy were running behind, though, so they were waiting on them before going farther. Grammy had called to tell Yeo that they had to go back for something at Mr. Chris's house. No one was heartbroken at the chance to eat a yummy breakfast.

"This gravy is different than yours, Yeo," Bennett said, stuffing another bite in his mouth. "It's so good."

"It's cowboy gravy," the waitress said. "It uses hamburger meat instead of sausage."

"Cowboy gravy? I have a cowboy," Bennett said happily. "I need this recipe."

Yeo giggled at Bennett, then eyed Caden out of the corner of his eye. His alpha talked with Carter about turning the attic into a room for Jimmy. It didn't sound like it would be too hard, and the two men were adorable with their heads close together, planning away. Jimmy and Summer were in a similar position, planning their comic book. Yeo's brother really did look just like him but with hot pink streaks through his black hair. He sent Yeo a shy smile when he caught him watching them. Hannah was busy entertaining Jake and Jules while Justin, Tanner, and Juan talked with Jackson.

"What do you make of that?" Bennett kept his voice low and nodded toward Yeo's papa and Ray.

They sat next to each other at the other end of the table. Yeo knew Dean was nervous about being in public. He let his long black hair fall into his face and at first had kept his eyes on the table. Ray hadn't seemed to like that. He'd held his chair for him when they'd come in and kept telling stupid jokes to make Dean laugh.

"What two letters in the alphabet are always jealous?" Ray leaned toward Dean and put an extra piece of bacon on his plate.

Dean looked at the beta, eyes exasperated.

"You are so silly." He picked up the bacon and bit into it. "Well? What two letters are always jealous?"

"NV," Ray said with relish. Dean giggled, dark eyes lighting up. He startled at the sound coming from his lips, looking shocked. Yeo didn't think his papa got the chance to laugh very often.

"Well?" Bennett leaned close to Yeo. "Ray's a good guy, but I'd swear he was flirting, not just helping a friend relax."

"I don't know," Yeo said, thoughtfully. "I don't know Papa well enough yet to be able to tell." His phone pinged with a text, and he read through it. "Papa, Grammy and Gramps want to talk to you and me outside." He grabbed Caden's hand. "We'll be right back. Will you order them some breakfast. Grammy said they aren't picky."

"Of course, angel," Caden said, kissing him gently. "Do you want me to come with you?"

Yeo shook his head. "We'll be fine, baby. Keep planning Jimmy's dream room."

Yeo and Dean walked outside the tiny diner and headed for Gramps and Grammy's truck. The older couple stood beside the trailer carrying two of the horses and some of the smaller animals. They looked concerned.

"Hey," Yeo said. "Are you all alright?"

"We left our number with your neighbor when we first left with everyone else," Grammy said. "He called us about an hour out with some troubling news. We went back, but things are a bit complicated."

"What's wrong?" Dean grabbed Yeo's hand. "We can go with Yeo, right?"

"You definitely can," Gramps said. "We're taking you home, and you'll love it. There's no question of that."

"The problem is with your dead husband," Grammy

said. "That man doesn't deserve to be called an alpha. He doesn't deserve to be called a man."

"What did he do?" Yeo squeezed his papa's hand. Whatever it was, they were together now. They could handle anything.

"You know he was cheating on you, right?" Gramps's eyes were both sympathetic and pissed off.

"Yes," Dean said in a small voice. "All my boys are omegas, and I can't have anymore babies. Jules's birth was really hard."

"He wanted an alpha," Grammy said.

"My boys are perfect," Dean said. "Alpha, omega, beta – it doesn't matter."

"You're right," Gramps said. "There are weak and horrible people of all genders and designations."

"What did he do?" Dean looked so sad.

"He caught a young omega alone and raped him," Gramps said bluntly.

"No." Dean shook his head, face full of horror and pain.

"Oh god," Yeo said, hugging his papa to him. "Ray said he was good-looking enough to talk a lot of men and women into bed."

"Rape isn't about sex," Dean whispered. "It's about control and power. I never thought he'd do that to other people."

"'Other people?' Papa, did that fucker rape you?" Yeo wanted to throw up.

Dean buried his face into Yeo's neck. "Do you hate me?"

"Why the hell would I hate you? I love you, Papa. Nothing he did would ever change that."

"I know it's off topic, Dean, but I was wondering about something. Based on all that Caden and Yeo have told us, I never understood why you would choose to have an affair with Michael Cook," Grammy said.

"I didn't… I didn't choose to," Dean said, tears falling against Yeo's skin. "No one believed me but Fawn."

"Papa," Yeo said, hugging him tighter. "Oh, Papa."

"Why didn't you abort him," a male voice asked. Yeo looked up, and Dean turned around. A very pregnant omega stood next to Gramps's truck. The back door of the extended cab stood open.

"Abort Yeo? I couldn't do that," Dean said. "I know it's different for every victim, but I loved Yeo as soon as I knew he grew in my belly. I was going to put him up for adoption since I didn't think I could take care of him. Fawn came to talk to me. She believed me about *him*. She told me she'd take care of Yeo and give him everything their wealth could. She'd make sure he was taken care of and treated as more than an omega. That was my choice."

"I can't stand the thought of it inside me," the young man said softly. "I know it's a baby, and it's innocent. I didn't want to abort it, but it's so hard. Every day, my body isn't my body. It's his."

"Simon raped you?" Dean met the man's gaze. "My alpha hurt you?"

"Yes," the man said roughly. "I wouldn't leave the

bar with him. I embarrassed him. He followed me outside." He swallowed. "It was over fast."

"I'm so sorry," Dean said, pulling out of Yeo's arm and walking closer to the man. "I should have stopped him."

"How? Everyone knows you tried, but the cops ignored you. Your parents didn't care. Everyone in the neighborhood knows that."

"It wasn't your fault either," Yeo said softly.

"I shouldn't have left the bar by myself," the man said. "I knew the street lights were out, and it was dangerous."

"No," Yeo said. "You should be able to go wherever you want and not worry about being attacked. This is all completely on Simon Wagner." He looked at his papa. "Only on Simon Wagner."

Dean returned to Yeo's arms, shuddering as he cried.

"What do you need?" Dean asked the man. "Wait. What's your name?"

"Logan," the man said. "I don't want the baby. I don't want to hurt him or her, but I can't take care of it. I don't want to. My mom and dad fully support any decision I make. They even offered to take it, but I don't want to see it every day. I feel horrible saying all that, but I just can't do it. My boyfriend even said we could raise it together. Everyone is ready to love it but me."

"That is fully understandable," Grammy said. "There's nothing wrong with how you feel."

"Do they know what he did?" Yeo had a good idea why someone would shoot the bastard now.

"Yes," Logan said. His eyes darted away. "My dad…"

"You don't have to say anything," Yeo said quickly. "The asshole got what he deserved."

"Very true," Dean agreed. He took a deep breath. "I'll take the baby. If you will give birth, I'll take care of the baby. I wish I would have kept my Yeo, but my parents had too much control of me. I can care for him or her."

Logan shuddered and leaned against the truck. "Thank you, thank you, thank you. Adoption was an option, but I went to school with Jackson. He's a good guy, and I wanted this baby to know its brothers. Everyone knows you're a good dad. I would worry if it was some stranger."

"We offered to take the baby too," Gramps said. "You don't *have* to take him or her in, Dean."

"Thank you, Gramps," Dean said, tearfully. "I can do it though." He looked to Yeo. "Well, I should ask you and Caden first, right? We'll be living in Caden's cabin."

"It's your cabin, Papa," Yeo said. "Caden said so. There's no need to ask us."

"I'll make it work," Dean said. "I can do this. I'll find a job in Hobson Hills and be near my Yeo."

"We'll do this together," Yeo said, kissing his papa's forehead. "We're a family."

"Logan is going to come with us to have the baby," Grammy said. "He'll stay with us."

"I'm due in two weeks," Logan said. "My boyfriend drives a truck, and he's going to meet me up there and stay with me until it's over. Gramps and Grammy said he could stay with them too."

"I can't imagine it any other way," Yeo said, smiling at the older couple.

"We'll go get some breakfast and let you two talk," Grammy said. She took Logan's hand, and they went into the diner.

"Papa, I love you," Yeo said. "I always will, but I wish you would have told me about what Michael Cook did to you. I looked up to him and loved him. I did everything I could to make him proud of me. If I had known what he did to you, I wouldn't have wasted my time on him."

"I wanted you to be happy and well cared for," Dean said. "I know myself better now. I would have managed raising you by myself. I wouldn't have married that asshole." He laughed. "I don't curse, Yeo. Look at me now."

"You wild man, you," Yeo said with a smile.

"I need a job," Dean said. "I don't know if I can work with people though. I have a hard time talking to strangers."

"We'll come up with something," Yeo said.

"I have an idea," Carter said. Yeo turned around and Carter, Ray, and Caden were there. They wore identical sheepish looks. "We eavesdropped."

"I'm sorry, angel. I looked out the window and saw Dean upset," Caden said.

"It's not like any of it will stay a secret," Dean said, shrugging. He lay his head on Yeo's shoulder. "What's your idea, Carter?"

"You like farming and animals, right?"

"Yes," Dean said. "I'm good at it, even if I'm a bit slow."

"My friend Ernie has an alpaca herd that he takes care of. He also teaches elementary school, so he has a hard time keeping up with them and his job. He was talking about hiring someone to do the morning feeding," Carter said.

"Ernie is Gramps and Grammy's grandson," Ray said. "He's a good guy. Noah is another one of their grandkids, and he's opening a horse therapy camp for veterans. He said he wanted someone part-time to help care for the horses."

"I think you'll find plenty of work, Papa," Yeo said. "Hobson Hills needs someone like you."

He didn't mention that he would be paying to help support his family too. He'd had a talk with Jackson, and they had a plan. Simon Wagner had gone out of his way to make sure his omega couldn't survive easily on his own. His children would quite happily help him, even with a new brother or sister on the way.

Dean took a deep breath. "Thank you, boys. I love animals, and I actually enjoy working. Both of those jobs sound perfect." He shook his head. "I've never had so many people try to help me before. I don't know what I did to deserve this, but I won't let you all down."

"Everyone deserves family and friends," Yeo said. "Soon enough, you'll be settled in at home, and everything will fall into place."

"Carter, we need Jimmy's room fixed fast," Caden said. "Dean's new baby will need its own room. Jules and Jake can share a room, or we could add an addition in the spring. An addition would be nice, wouldn't it?"

"I know just the spot," Carter said excitedly. "We could just make a new master bedroom and bath. Put it right on the back, facing the lake."

"I'll text Harper now," Ray said. "The baby will need furniture. I'll go by the thrift store when we get home, but the baby should have nice things. Ernie said they fixed the boys' rooms up nice with some pieces Harper had stockpiled."

Yeo and Dean stared at each other a minute before laughing. "See, Papa? We're in this together, whether you like it or not."

# CHAPTER 15

Caden watched Carter paint long, smooth strokes on the wall of Jimmy's attic room.

"Why don't my brushstrokes look like that?" He had been banned from painting after his second try.

"You got the writing skills in the family, son," Caden's dad said. "Carter and Jimmy got the painting skills."

"I got the beauty and the brains in the family," Cain said, smugly. The whole Benson clan had rushed to get to Maine when they'd heard what happened with Yeo's papa. It had just been a week, but Jimmy's room was basically done.

"I can't believe this is all for me," Jimmy said. He crawled along the floor, painting the trim. "I've never had my own room before. This place is going to be amazing."

"I've seen the start of that comic you and Summer are working on," Cain said. "Your room isn't the only amazing thing." He shook his head. "I've never even dreamed of being so creative. You, Summer, and Caden are all so damn talented."

"All my boys are," John said. He looked fondly at Jimmy. "All of them. I'll miss seeing you every day, Cain, but I'm glad your mother and I are moving up here. We'll be right next to our boys."

Jimmy grinned. "Jake can't wait to go fishing with you and Olive. Plus, you promised to teach me to drive. Jackson and Papa gave up already, but you promised."

"You can't be worse than Cain," John said.

"I wasn't bad," Cain protested. "Anyway, you're forgetting the most important part. Mother will be right next to her new BFF."

The Bensons shared a grin.

"Mother took to Dean like Bennett took to Yeo," Caden said.

"Darling," Susan called from downstairs. "Surely it doesn't take five people to paint four walls. Send someone downstairs to help us move this couch."

Everyone in the Wilson and Benson family had found some piece of furniture or decoration to donate to the Wagner family. Caden had never been prouder of his parents and brothers. Cain had even shipped a large painting from Georgia for Dean. He said the sweet and simple nature scene reminded him of fresh starts. Dean had cried.

Caden left Jimmy and Carter painting and headed downstairs with Cain. They dodged two cats on the steps but managed to stay upright. Susan and Dean were waiting in the living room. Dean's dog, Beau, sat at his feet, watching the omega adoringly. The golden retriever loved his person and followed Dean everywhere he went. Caden had wanted to cry when he saw Dean and the boys reunited with all their pets. Jackson was even able to have his dog and cat with him at his new place. The owner was very understanding. Very.

The owner was Gramps.

"Caden, where do you think the couch should go? Should it face the television or the fireplace?" Dean looked so grave and concerned. Caden would have laughed, but he'd quickly figured out that Dean had never been allowed to have an opinion. What seemed so simple to Caden was a huge hurdle for the omega. Physical abuse was just part of what he'd suffered while married to Simon.

"Which seat will you use the most here?" The living room set Barry had given Dean and his boys was brown leather. It included a huge couch and two very comfortable-looking recliners.

Dean thought for a minute, nibbling his lip. "The recliner is more comfortable for my leg."

"Alright," Caden said. "Would you watch television more or would you read in front of the fire more?"

"Read," Dean said. He didn't have to think about that.

"Why don't we put the couch toward the television and the chairs toward the fireplace?"

Dean smiled widely. "Perfect! It's like a big square space."

Susan wrapped an arm around Dean's shoulder. "I love it, Dean. Why don't you and I go to the kitchen and see what Grey is cooking? It smells delicious. My boys can arrange the furniture here."

"Okay," Dean said and followed Susan from the living room.

"I thought you were crazy when I heard you were giving the cabin away," Cain said, voice low. Caden and his brother started moving the couch. "The more I learned about Dean and what he's been through, the more I understood it. He's why I wanted to be a lawyer. No one should feel like they have no choice."

"I love him," Caden said. "He's Yeo's papa, yes, but he's such a sweet man. I caught him singing to Jules the other day. Jules fell outside on the ice and hurt his ankle. Dean carried him inside, limp and all, and dried his tears and patched up his ankle. He sang this sweet song the whole time, and Jules forgot he hurt."

Cain smiled softly. "He sounds like an amazing father."

They each moved one of the chairs to the right spot, then arranged the matching side table and coffee table Grey and Harper had brought for the family.

"I heard that someone else is going to be a dad in about six months."

Caden blinked. "Fuck. I forgot to tell you."

Cain's mouth dropped open. "You just cursed." He shook his head in amazement. "Caden Benson just cursed."

"I don't believe it," John said, trotting down the stairs to the attic that Carter had put in a few days ago. "Caden is the best behaved of all of you."

"He did," Cain said. He smirked at Caden. "He also forgot to tell us about Yeo being pregnant."

John looked disgruntled. "I heard about it from Zoe, Caden. Really. You need to communicate more, son. At least your mother and I are moving up here. What will Cain do? Will you just forget to tell him everything?"

"Do we need another intervention?" Juan asked with a grin. The man carried an armful of dog and cat beds. Dean and the boys had two dogs and three cats. Luckily, they were all house trained, even though the asshole alpha hadn't let them keep them inside.

Cain snickered. "I heard that you and Carter had some trouble. How is it you can live in the same small town as each other but still manage to avoid one another?"

"Neither of them talks," Juan said. He started setting out the pet beds. "You must have gotten all the speaking ability in the family, man."

"I am rather amazing," Cain said thoughtfully.

"You're so modest too, son," John said wryly.

"Caden," Jules said, walking into the room. He held Linc's hand. "Will you help us put Huckleberry in his new outfit. He's all wiggly."

"You bet," Caden said, ignoring the snickers coming from the men around him. "That sweater you and Ernie made is really cute. I know Huck will like it once he gets used to it."

"He's cold without his hair," Jules said, grabbing Caden's hand with his free one and tugging him back toward the boys' room. They had recently cut Huck's hair to give to Ernie to make yarn. "Ernie said he'd save all Huckleberry's hair and make him something special out of it."

"That's a good idea," Caden said. He helped the boys get Huck in his new sweater. Then they visited with Jules's hamsters. After a few minutes, Linc started yawning. Together, Caden and Jules read the little boy to sleep. He curled into Jules's bed, and Jake's beagle, Lola, hopped up and cuddled against him.

"Lola likes to cuddle," Jules whispered. He held Huckleberry in his arms and looked up at Caden. "I'm hungry."

"Grey is making something yummy for lunch. Let's go see what we can snag." Caden wrapped his arm around the boy's thin shoulders, and they headed to the kitchen.

The kitchen was busy. Grey and his abuela, Ines, were rolling out shells. It looked like they were going to make quesadillas. Grammy and Gramps sat in the kitchen nook, cuddled together. They were looking at something on a laptop. Bennett and Yeo sat with them, a plate of crackers and cheese between them. Jules headed straight for his brother.

Caden stood frozen in the doorway, watching his mother laugh and dance with Dean. Soft music played from someone's phone, and Susan and Dean twirled around the kitchen, giggling and smiling as they tripped over one another. Yeo ambled over to him, tucking up against his side.

"They're really something, huh?"

"I've never seen Mother act like that before," Caden

whispered. "Her and Father dance perfectly together. She's always… perfect."

She wasn't too perfect now. Her hair was out of place, and her face was red with laughter.

"I like it."

"Me too. Papa needed a friend like her. I think she needed him too," Yeo said.

"Yes," Caden said and dropped a kiss on Yeo's head. "I'm so glad I saw you that day, angel. I don't want to think about life without you and the kids in it. Everything about you makes my life better, brighter."

"I brought a lot of drama, baby," Yeo said. "Are you sure you don't mind it all?"

"It's not drama," Caden said. "It's family. Sometimes family can be messy, but it's worth it. Dean and your brothers are what we all needed, not just you and me. Mother needed a best friend to be silly with, and Father needed some more kids to spoil."

"Jackson needed a new job," Yeo said. "He loves the bookstore almost as much as I do."

"He likes his new place too," Caden said, smiling at the memory of the omega's face when he'd seen the small, two-bedroom house Gramps had found him. It was right next-door to Ines and was perfect for him and his two pets. "I'm glad it's close to us."

"How does Gramps know about all the good deals in town?"

"The man knows everything," Caden said. "Don't bother questioning it."

"Do you know what he's doing right now?" Yeo

nodded toward the kitchen table. Caden noticed Jules had polished off the cheese and crackers.

"What?"

"He's putting in a bid on the twenty acres of forest between here and your parents' cabin."

"Why? I didn't even know it was for sale."

"It wasn't. The owner knows Gramps, though, and had no plans for the land."

"What does Gramps want it for?"

"I have no idea," Yeo said. "He just said that the family is growing, so we need to be prepared." He looked at Caden. "Are we Wilsons? If we are, I didn't know we were."

"I'm fairly certain we're honorary Wilsons," Caden said. "How would you feel about being a Benson?"

Yeo's black eyes widened, then sparkled with joy. "Would Linc and Summer be Bensons too?"

"Of course," Caden said.

"Then sign me up," Yeo said. He laid his head on Caden's shoulder, and together, they watched his papa dance around the kitchen.

eo watched Carter and Elijah kiss. Caden stood with the rest of the wedding party, and he looked damn fine in his black tux. The couple's formal wedding was beautiful, but not because of the flowers, ribbons, and other decorations. The way Carter watched Elijah made Yeo's heart beat fast while the way Elijah's eyes warmed when the traced over Carter's face made Yeo sniffle. The two men loved one another, and it was obvious.

"I now present to you, Mr. and Mr. Benson," the pastor said. The crowd cheered, and Olive ran and jumped into Carter's arms. Her pretty dress fluttered around her, and the basket she carried trailed rose petals. "The new couple are hosting a reception at The Irish Rose. The address is listed on your invitation, but please let one of the ushers know if you need directions.

Yeo picked up his youngest brother, Min, and took Linc's hand. Dean had taken great pleasure in giving the youngest addition to their family a Korean name. Min was an omega and belonged to Dean, one hundred percent. Yeo grinned and herded Summer and his brothers down the aisle. Jackson and his papa were back at the pub, helping Grey and the others cook for the reception. Caden met him at the door.

"Are you all ready for the food?" He picked up Linc and gave his boy a cuddle.

They all cheered.

"Do you even need to ask," Yeo said, kissing his alpha. "You look so handsome in that tux."

"Eww," Summer said. "See how they're looking at each other? I told you guys it was horrible."

"They love each other," Jules said. "It's sweet."

Yeo kissed the top of his little brother's head.

"Gag," Jimmy said. "It's too sweet."

Jake just laughed at them. "Come on. I'm hungry."

"You're always hungry," Yeo said.

By the time they reached the newly remodeled pub, most of the guests were already there. Abel and Justin had gone all out and renovated the place beautifully. The pub looked completely different from the dump it had started as. It was larger and had a patio area so people could bring their pets with them to lunch. From what Justin had told Yeo, they planned on making it a real pub, not just a bar. They had already hired a cook and were interviewing bartenders and servers. Yeo had a feeling the place was going to be amazing.

For the wedding reception, the two men had set out long buffet-style tables and loaded them down with delicious food. A live band was already playing, and Carter and Elijah slow danced on the dance floor.

"They look so beautiful together," Yeo said, squeezing Caden's hand. "I'm glad you and your brother got your heads out of your asses."

Jules and Jake laughed, and Summer rolled her eyes.

"It really did take you guys long enough," she said. "Oh, there's Hannah. I'm going to ask her to dance."

"We've lost Summer for the rest of the reception," Jimmy said dryly. He smiled softly as he watched the two girls. "They look cute together, don't they?"

"Mr. Ray is going to ask Papa to dance today too," Jules said. "I heard him say so."

"Hmm," Jimmy said. "Papa sure does blush anytime Mr. Ray is around."

"He's not like Dad was," Jake said. "I like him."

"Me too," Yeo said.

Caden couldn't stop his grin when he saw Ray at the edge of the crowd. He kept fiddling with his bowtie, but it was crooked. His friend, Mr. Bartley, stood beside the beta and finally smacked his hands away, fixing the bowtie in seconds.

Dean stepped out of the kitchen with a platter of appetizers in his hand. He froze when he saw Ray and blushed when the man rushed over and whispered in his ear. Mr. Bartley grabbed the tray with a wink and brought it to the buffet table. Ray pulled Yeo's papa to the dancefloor.

"Well," Yeo said. "Would you look at that?"

"Papa looks beautiful out there," Jules said. "He loves dancing."

"He does," Caden said. "Now, who wants food?"

"There's no time to eat, Caden," Grey said, running to his friend, Abel and Justin right behind him. "The Hot Mess Club is ready to dance."

They pulled Caden out to the dance floor, and Yeo laughed as the four men danced together.

"Do you need some help?" Tanner asked, shaking his head. "My boyfriend abandoned me for his friends."

"What a coincidence," Yeo said. "My fiancé did the same thing. Let's go eat our heartache away."

LATER THAT NIGHT, Yeo slipped into bed beside Caden. His feet hurt, but he had enjoyed dancing the afternoon away. Caden's arms slipped around him, and Yeo laid his head on his alpha's chest.

"Caden?"

"Yes, angel? What's wrong? You've been acting a little off since we got home."

"Fawn, Lowell, and Derek are coming to visit next month," Yeo said. "I'm going to talk to them about Michael." Yeo hadn't called the man *dad* since he found out the fucker raped Dean. "He deserves to pay for what he did to Papa. I don't know what to do for sure though."

"You're right," Caden said. "He's paying already, but if something can be done, we should do it."

"What do you mean 'he's paying already?' The company is struggling, but it'll even out."

"He's lost you, Summer, Derek, and Lowell," Caden

said. "They all know what he did to Dean and any respect they had left for the man is long gone. Fawn stays with him, but only for the money. He knows that. He has nothing but money and his company. That may seem like a lot, but it's really not."

"Lowell doesn't plan on even trying to get involved in the company," Yeo said. "Derek started his landscaping company. I think you're right. He's lost his kids."

"What's the most important thing to you, angel?"

"Our family," Yeo said with no hesitation. "You, Linc, Summer, Papa and my brothers, our friends, and our pets."

"Michael and Richard Cook have nothing. They have no family, no friends," Caden said.

Yeo was silent for a moment.

"They really don't have anything." He kissed Caden. "We have everything, don't we?"

"Yes," Caden said. "We don't need a family company and a fortune. We could live in a desolate town and a broken house, but as long as we had each other, we'd be fine."

"You're right," Yeo agreed. "I'm glad our town isn't desolate, and our home isn't broken though."

Caden laughed. "Me too." He covered Yeo's small baby bump with his hand. "I can't wait until our daughter is born."

"Me neither," Yeo said. "Min soothed my baby fever a little bit, but I want our daughter."

"Do you think Logan will be okay?"

"His boyfriend and his parents are really supportive. I think he'll be just fine," Yeo said.

He thought of the young man. He'd left as soon as Min was born. The omega had not been interested in being a part of the baby boy's life, but Yeo understood why. He hoped he would be able to heal with time.

Yeo considered the look in Ray's eyes when he watched Dean. "I think Michael Cook made some enemies this year. He isn't an honest business man. I had to clean up a lot of his messes. I have a feeling he'll get what's coming to him."

# OTHER M/M ROMANCE BOOKS BY C.W. GRAY

**The Blue Solace Series** – science fiction/fantasy, mpreg

1. The Mercenary's Mate – https://amzn.to/2MAOFEH
2. The General's Mate – https://amzn.to/2G1abRE
3. The Soldier's Mate – https://amzn.to/2S7R6ng
4. The Lieutenant's Mate – https://amzn.to/2THZ47w
5. The Engineer's Mate – https://amzn.to/2HpI4vH
6. The Captain's Mate – https://amzn.to/2knP03W
7. The Rebel's Mate – *Coming Soon*
8. Fire's Mate – *Coming Soon*

**The Hobson Hills Omegas** – non-shifter, mpreg, omegaverse

1. Falling for the Omega – https://amzn.to/2BgWURV
2. Snow Kisses for My Omega – https://amzn.to/2TdDiol
3. Romancing the Omega – https://amzn.to/2UNENKD
4. Healing the Omega – https://amzn.to/2FNcXrY
5. A Pint for my Omega – https://amzn.to/2XItQf7
6. Unraveling the Omega – https://amzn.to/2xRCnRL
7. The Alpha's Christmas Wish – *Coming December 2019*

**Hobson Hills Shorts** – short stories from the world of Hobson Hills Omegas

1. The Beta's Love Song – https://amzn.to/2UrRPNN
2. Bennett's Dream – https://amzn.to/2GwSpG3
3. Justin's Journey – https://amzn.to/2DhW1t1
4. Grey's Gift – https://amzn.to/2BcjxXf
5. Hobson Hills Shorts: Volume One – https://amzn.to/2M3oGGZ

**The Silver Isles** – paranormal, mermen, mpreg

1. The Guppy Prince – *Coming Soon*
2. The Not so Little Merman – *Coming Soon*
3. The Sea Witch – *Coming Soon*

If you would like to keep up with releases, please like and follow me on Instagram (@c.w._gray) or Facebook (@cwgrayauthor), join C.W. Gray's Reading Nook on Facebook, or visit my website at https://cwgray-author.com.